I0699121
THE
VENGEANCE
OF
ALARI
A REALMS OF ELSWYTH STANDALONE
WILLOW ASTERIA

# The Vengeance of Alari

Willow Asteria

# Content Warning

Please be advised that this book may not be suitable for all audiences.

This book contains sexual content, mention of past sexual assault, mention of spiked drinks, mention of physical emasculation as a form of retribution and punishment, death, blood, graphic violence, and other topics some readers may not find suitable.

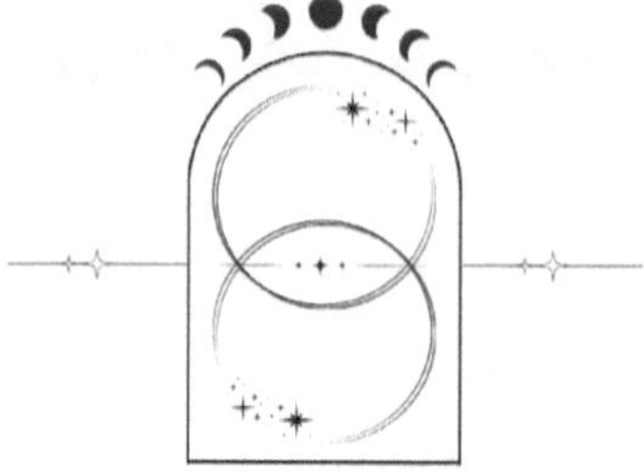

# Realms of Elswyth

In the land of Elswyth, six portals exist that lead to the fae realms.

Orilon. Irolyth. Alari. Aeros. Khaldon. Tarak.

ELSWYTH
THE HUMAN REALM
VARIA
ZAMORA
MAGLA
CALDOR
PENDRIL
PORTAL
TO
ANOTHER REALM

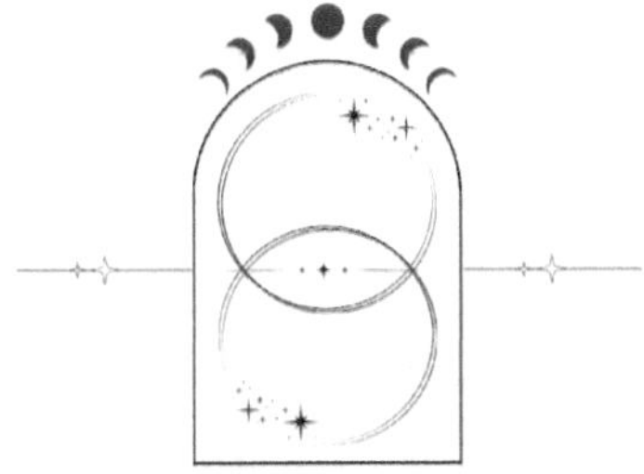

# One

Today marks sixty years since the King of Alari vanished. Arik Tristian Delmari left the castle one day with the royal family's trident. To this day, no one knows where he went or why. Before he left, he gave his twin sister, Ariella, the Gem of Alari. The Gem had been embedded in the trident and the two have never been separated in all of Alari's history, until then. Stories were told that the trident was given to the first king of Alari, Triton Marrion Delmari, by The Mother and her daughter Nera when they first split the realms and created the merfolk. The trident was to keep us safe, and the Gem was what gave it its magic. It, too, vanished over the years.

No one outside the royal family speaks of the king who stole our trident. He was removed from Alari's history. Even saying his name would get you banished from our kingdom. The Queen, Ariella Delphina Delmari, gave no one-second chances. When you were exiled, it was a death sentence.

Years later, the Princess was born, and it was discovered she had the gift of voice. With her voice, she could influence or cause pain to others. The Queen used that to her advantage. For the last twenty years, the princess's voice has been used to force the people to forget about Arik entirely.

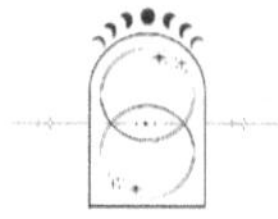

I was so tired of being my mother's puppet. A gut feeling was told my uncle did not leave of his own accord. Could my mother have something to do with his disappearance so that she could steal the crown? I was tired of her using me— using my voice to make the people of Alari forget my uncle. For the past year, I've been sneaking around the castle, trying to prove it. So far, I haven't found anything of use. Everything about him had been removed from the royal library, and not even in my mother's private writings did she mention him. Even though I had found nothing so far, I refused to give up.

Late at night, once the castle was silent and all but a few guards had gone to bed, I snuck out of my room and swam back down to the library. There was a single shelf left of books that I had not combed through. If I didn't find anything on this last shelf, I did not know where I was going to look next. I bent down to grab the first one off the shelf and noticed that some of them stuck out more than others. When I examined them closer, I saw a small journal stuffed behind the tomes. As I pulled it out, I was startled by a voice from behind.

"Princess Calliope? What are you doing here so late?"

I spun and met the eyes of our royal archivist, Varun.

Quickly, I grabbed a few more books off the shelf to hide the notebook I found. "Oh, I couldn't sleep and figured I would take some of these back to my room tonight for some late-night time reading," I said nervously.

"I did not know you were a reader. The only time I have ever seen you in the library is during your lessons when you were a child." His eyes lit up as he spoke.

"I do not have time during the day to stop by, and I don't like getting in the way. I will return these in the morning!" Not wanting to be questioned further, I started to swim past him.

"Wait!" He stuck out his bright yellow tail to block my path.

I swallowed hard. "Yes?"

"I see you have the work of Lyric Kai. Have you read anything under her other pen name, L.K. Wake?"

"I have not. I will have to check out those works tomorrow when I return." I smiled.

He moved his tail. "Let me not keep you any longer. Good night, princess."

I wished Varun a good night and raced to my chambers. As soon as I was inside, I locked the door behind me and pulled out the journal. Many pages had been ripped out, and others had barely legible scribblings. The first page that made any sense had only one sentence on it.

'My name is King Arik Delmari. I will make Alari great again.'

Flipping through the pages, I saw a drawing of a mermaid and arrows pointing to the next page. It showed the same mer but with legs instead of a tail. The following page detailed how the mer could transform into bi-pedal creatures to travel on land. There were more ripped-out pages, and then a page covered in scribbles to the point it was almost blacked out. The last two pages were a drawing of a cave that had six portals. Each was labeled, and the one marked 'Elswyth' was circled over and over. The final page was a map detailing how to get to the cave.

I smiled as I studied the map. This had to be where my uncle went. I had to find him. I had to bring him home so I could prove that my mother was up to no good. She refused to tell me why my uncle had to be forgotten by the people.

I vowed to make them remember.

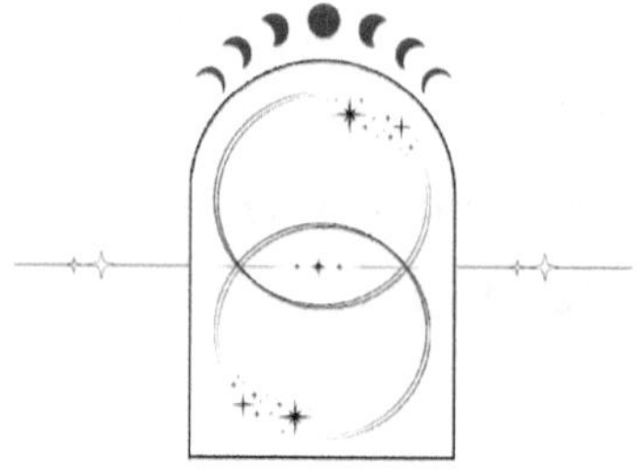

# Two

The next night, I was ready to go on my adventure. Once the lights in the town below went dark, I swam off my balcony and into the open ocean. The map showed landmarks to look out for, and which direction to go. The first landmark was a large coral reef. Once the coral forked into three paths, I was to follow the third path. Continuously, I looked behind me and watched as the castle got smaller and smaller. Anxiety welled in my core. How long would it be until the queen sent guards looking for me?

Eventually, I found the second landmark, a ship. Before the fae realms were split, all the fae lived together. Now we were all in our own realms, with little contact with one another. This ship was from that time. Now nothing lived above the waters of Alari, as it was now an endless ocean. The ship was now almost all gone and was overgrown with barnacles, algae, and coral. Fish swam in and out of the ship, over the years it had been turned into their home. A golden mermaid statue sat straight up out of the sand. Her arm was extended, and I swam in the direction of her pointed finger. I let out a yawn as I pushed myself forward. Traveling for hours without stopping was beginning to take its toll. Finally, the last landmark came into view, and a second wave of energy hit me. I looked down at the giant trench beneath me. My heart pounded in my chest as I stared into the darkness.

Was I making the right choice? Is this truly where I was to go? Or was this a trap set by whoever really left this journal?

I traveled all this way, no reason to turn tail and run now. Without a second thought, I swam down into the total darkness. The farther I swam, the more nervous I got. Stopping the descent, I looked back up and realized how far I traveled. The sun now illuminated the world above. Morning had come to Alari. It would not be long until mother had her guards searching the ocean for me.

Looking back down, I mustered all the courage I could. Could I find my way through the inky blackness before I found what I was looking for? I started my swim downward again, and the trench narrowed. It was now only wide enough to fit two merfolk.

Just as I thought I needed to travel back up to get a better view now that the sun was up, I was caught up in a strong current. I tried to fight against it, but it just caused me to flip and tumble over my tail. As I reached out to grab hold of the side wall, the rocks slipped out of my grasp. All I could do was allow the current to take me. It eventually had to stop, right? I turned to see that I was headed straight for the wall of the trench. I reached its end. The water had not slowed down a bit, and I was about to be slammed directly into the jagged rocks.

Just before I smashed into them, my body was pushed downward by another strong stream. Tumbling through the water, the trench continued straight down. I fell for what seemed like an eternity in the all-consuming darkness. The undertow slowed, and my body hit soft sand. The forceful waters vanished. I shivered from the icy temperature, above the trench the waters were warm. I was not used to the cold. Looking around, I was in a cave with red translucent crystals sticking out from the dark stone. They gave off a soft glow that illuminated the space. I reached into my bag, thankful it didn't get yanked away from me. Pulling out the journal, I looked at the red crystals drawn on the map. All I needed to do was go through the opening on the opposite side of the cave and it would take me exactly where I needed to go. I was so close to finding the portals. Rising from the ground, I brushed the sand off my scales and pushed my loose hair out of my face.

Ringing filled my ears as I swam down the path. I prayed to The Mother that at the end of this tunnel I would find what I was looking for just as the map showed.

Endless twists and turns snaked their way through the dark stone, the only light was from the red glow of the gems. Just when I thought I would never leave the tunnel, it opened up to a large circular room. Unlike where I started, white glowing crystals jutted out of the ceiling. The tunnel I came from was the only entrance into the space. Embedded in the walls were six white arches. At the top of each arch was carved the name of each realm in the ancient language of the fae. Though I do not speak it fluently, I recognized some of the words as it is still used in some of our religious texts and rituals. Each archway was filled with different colored smoke. Orilon was purple. Irolyth was red. Aeros was white. Khaldon was brown. Tarak was yellow.

When I came to Elswyth's arch, I was not met with smoke. I stared back at my own reflection. It rippled as if it was made from silver water. I stared into my blue eyes as I pushed back my dark navy hair. The white lights gave my ice-blue tail a silver sheen. Once I went through this portal, everything would change. Would

I even recognize the person I transformed into? What type of world would I enter? I could not imagine a world not underwater. My mind could not even picture what such a world would look like. It was now or never.

To free Alari from my mother, I would face the unknown.

With that last thought, I swam through the portal.

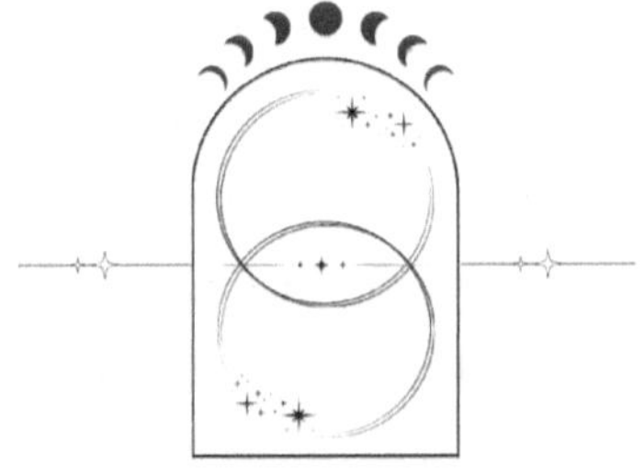

# Three

On the other side of the portal I found myself surround-ed by warm water. I was in a dark cylinder-shaped space, and the only way to go was up unless I wanted to go back through the portal. The water here had a strange green hue I had never seen. The ocean of Alari was all blue.

Propelling upward, I finally breached the surface, throwing my head back to get my hair out of my face. To my surprise, it was nighttime. Either I was in the cave for longer than I thought, or this realm was on a differ-ent time. Looking around, I found I was surrounded by sandy dunes and beach grass. I pulled myself out of the small pool of water and sat on the sandy shore. Closing my eyes, I tried to focus my magic. The journal did not provide any information on how to transform. Before finding the journal, I did not even know that was a thing that the merfolk could do. All I could do was force my magic to work in ways it never had before and prayed that it worked. A tingling sensation took over the base of my tail as if it was going numb. I opened my eyes and let out a huff of air when nothing had happened, and I splashed my tail in the water. Trying one more time, I did not even feel the tingle of magic.

I looked up into the night sky, focusing on the full moon overhead. Throwing my prayers to The Mother once again, I begged for her to help me. To allow me to shed my tail and gain two legs. Allow me to walk, to be a part of this unknown world. I closed my eyes once again to focus. My magic welled inside me, and my entire body tingled. The sensation of the water bubbling around my bottom half overwhelmed my senses. When the bubbling stopped, I opened my eyes and looked down, a smile grew on my face. I lifted my right leg from the pool and watched as beads of water dripped from it.

Quickly, I jumped up, and a cry of joy escaped my throat. My legs wobbled as my bare feet hit solid ground for the first time. The soft sand got in between my toes, and I wiggled them in deeper. Once steady, I walked through the sand, down a path in between the dunes. The sweet and salty air filled my nose. Just beyond the white dunes was the shoreline. The ocean beyond the sand was almost black. Large, jagged rocks jetted from the dark waters. Far across the ocean, lights from a town glittered on the horizon. Truly, I was in awe. My thoughts drifted to the people who lived there. I had never met anyone who wasn't merfolk. I had read some pieces about non-mer in books, but there were very few of those available back home. Who were these people and what were they like?

Staring off into the ocean, there was something that felt so wrong about it. I wish I could put my finger on exactly what was calling this ill feeling. As the waves crashed onto the shore, I was careful not to allow the water to touch my skin. Following the shoreline, I learned I was on a small island surrounded by large rock formations. The longer I stayed on the island, the more the feeling of dread crept over me. I did not see a way out of the cave system in Alari. The current blocked my only path. I needed to find another way home. Could there be another portal somewhere in this strange land? Even if there was, that would require me to enter the sea that filled me with terror.

Who would have thought the Princess of the Mer would be afraid of the ocean?

The white sand transitioned into a slate of rock. A large wave crashed against it, and the water settled on top of the rock. My foot slipped on the slippery stone, causing me to fall. I was able to catch myself before my face smashed into the hard ground. However, one of my new legs was not so lucky. It had scraped against the rock, and blood now dripped down. I hobbled over to a spot where a clump of seaweed lay on the sand and sat next to it. Staring at the ocean, I hesitated. Fear rattled me as I reached down to touch it, and a shiver ran down my spine from the frigid temperature. I used the salt water from the sea to clean the wound, hissing as it made contact. Using the seaweed, I wrapped my leg to keep the cut clean. The waves crashed against the shore and washed away my blood.

Maybe this was a fool's errand. Maybe I should return home. Maybe this world was not meant for someone like me.

I pushed myself up and headed back toward the portal. There had to be a way out of the tunnel I found myself in. I could return home for a while, just until I had a better plan. Just as the portal came into view, I heard a deep and dark voice from behind me.

"It has been a long time since I have seen another from Alari."

I slowly spun to see a tall man with long blond hair staring back at me with dark blue eyes. He appeared human, but I had a strange feeling he wasn't. Water dripped off his bare body. We stood in silence for a moment before I responded. "Another?" It was the only word that would escape my lips.

Everything about this man screamed for me to run, from the darkness in his eyes to the predatory smirk on his face, but all I could do was stand there as he stepped closer.

"Yes. I once called Alari my home. Long before the Queen took over and betrayed me," he growled.

"Betrayed you?" Could this man have the answers I have been looking for?

He took another step forward, and I looked down to avoid his burning gaze. He grabbed me by my chin and forced me to look up at him. A chill ran down my body as his touch was like ice. "Yes. She stole something very precious to me." He stared at me intensely for a long silent moment. "You have her eyes." He dropped my chin and took a step back, giving me an up-and-down glance. "What brings you here? The human realm of Elswyth is not a place for young mermaids."

"I came looking for my uncle. I found his journal with a map showing the way to this place. I was hoping I could find him."

"And if you did find him? What would you do?" He raised his eyebrow and slowly circled me.

I spun in place, not wanting him out of my sight. "I want to know why he left. Why would he leave our people? Was it the Queen who chased him away? Did she make him disappear so the throne would be hers?"

He stopped and burst into laughter. "Do you think him to be some kind of hero? Someone who was banished for stopping a sea witch from destroying Alari? Let me tell you something about the Queen, princess." Large red tentacles appeared from behind him, coming out of his back. "She should have done a better job at keeping you away from me. Now that I have you, there is nothing that will stop me from finishing what I started."

I spun and ran toward the portal. Fuck, I should have brought something to defend myself with. Why did I not think of that? Just as I reached the small pool of green water, a tentacle wrapped around my ankle and yanked. I fell to the ground and hit it hard. My face planted into the sand, and it filled my mouth. Lifting my head, I tried to spit it out. Grabbing at the ground to hold myself in place, the grains just fell through my fingers. My skin burned as it scraped against the ground. Another tentacle wrapped around my waist and pulled me up into the air. Three more held my wrists and legs as I hung in the air in front of the man.

"Dear niece, please don't take any of this personally. It seems that what your mother stole from me is embedded within you. This won't be a pleasant removal, and you won't be able to return to Alari after I take it. Which is good news for me. We can't let the Queen know I am one step closer to my plan."

I could not believe the words that fell from his lips. I was not aware of anything embedded in me. The thought of not being able to return home nearly broke my heart. I could not allow that to happen.

"Arik! Let me go!" I screamed as I squirmed, trying to break free. "It doesn't have to be like this! I am sure whatever happened between you and mother can be resolved!"

My uncle chuckled under his breath. "I will take the Gem of Alari from your throat, steal back the trident from those pesky pirates, and then I will drown Elswyth and take it as the new home of the mer. You see, Alari is too small for us. We deserved better than what The Mother provided. I will make the mer great again, and it will all be mine."

All this time the missing Gem was within me. One of the most sacred relics of our people was within my possession. I couldn't help but wonder if that was where my gift of voice had come from. Or, was it a gift from the gods who had once given us our tails and home?

I opened my mouth to sing, hoping I could lure him to sleep and escape. Before the first note escaped my throat, a tentacle was shoved into my mouth.

"Not so fast. You don't think I would know Ariella's one trick? You cannot charm me, brat." The tentacle pushed its way down my throat. I choked hard on it as it forced its way in deeper. Just as quickly as it entered, it was pulled out, and I heaved as it was fully removed. Strands of drool connected me to the tentacle and the red gem that it now held in its grasp. Arik took the Gem and held it up in the moon's light and it glimmered. A wicked smile grew as he dropped me onto the ground, and a cold and empty feeling took over my entire body. I could not move. I could not speak.

"Well, I would say it was great meeting you, but in all honesty, you were quite a bore. I was hoping for more of a fight from someone who held the power of the Gem. Now that I have your power, say goodbye to any idea you have of returning home. Your shifting abilities are gone. Also, good luck getting off this island. No boats dare to come this far south, lest they wish to endure my wrath. Goodbye, dear niece. I am off to find the damn pirates who have my trident."

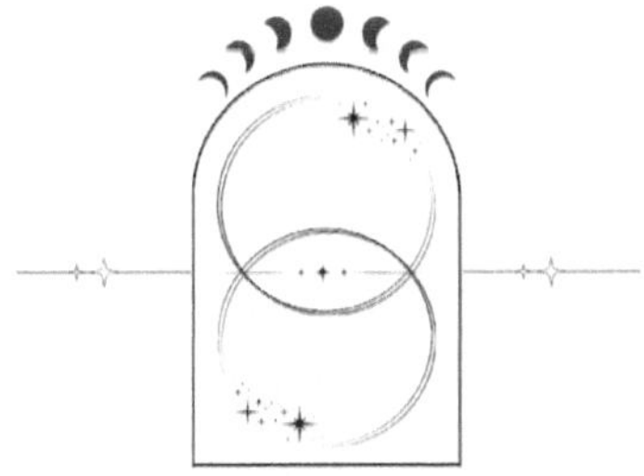

# Four

I laid on the sand for hours with tears streaming down my face. Each time I tried to scream from the pain, the sounds refused to escape my throat. After my uncle left, I dragged myself back to the pool. My magic refused to come to me as I tried to shift back to my tail. Just as Arik told me, nothing happened. I no longer could feel my magic. Emptiness filled my chest. A piece of me that I had held near and dear had been ripped from me.

How did the Gem of Alari end up inside me? Did mother know about that this entire time? Why would she not have told me? Maybe I would have been more careful if she had been honest about the fact that I held something so powerful and sacred to our people. If she knew Arik was a monster, why would she not tell me, or the kingdom? If I had known the truth about him, I would not have sought him.

Since I was left here, I floated in and out of consciousness. The sun peeked over the horizon and illuminated the island. Forcing myself up, I walked over to the shore, where the waves crashed onto my bare feet. I had hoped that the water would offer me comfort, but all it did was exaggerate the hollowness in my chest. Boats now floated on the ocean's surface, both large and small. All but one were far from the island. I stared at the large black ship as it got closer to me. Mounted in the front was a golden mermaid statue. I couldn't help but wonder how they knew what we looked like. The people of Alari had not been to Elswyth since before the splitting of the fae realms. Was there another community of mer still here in this strange realm? If there was, would they be able to help me return to Alari?

The large ship threw down an anchor just behind the large rocks. My eyes traveled up the ship to a man who stood on the bow. The sunlight made his dark skin glow. He grabbed the tip of his red and gold tricorn hat and tipped it to keep the sun from his golden eyes. Even from so far away, I swear they locked on to me before a grin grew on his face. He spun away and walked out of view. The sounds of men yelling could be heard from across the sea, but I could not make out the words they were saying.

Should I try to call out for them to help me? Ever since I arrived, I wanted to know what the people of this world were like. Now that I had my chance, I wasn't sure If I did. What if they were just as vile as my uncle? I had thought the best of him, and that turned out to be a huge mistake. Walking back toward the center of the island, I looked for anything I could use as a weapon.

Even though my entire body ached with sorrow and hollowness, I would not allow myself to be a victim ever again. Walking had become much easier, almost second nature.

There was nothing in the center of the island, so I continued to the far shore. I stood on the shoreline for a moment and looked out to the endless ocean. There was no land in sight. The cold water splashed against my feet, causing me to jump. It was time I returned to my search.

After a few minutes of searching, I found a large piece of wood that had washed ashore. The tip was pointed, as if it had been once a part of something else, but was snapped apart. I returned to the front of the island to watch the large ship again and was surprised to see a smaller boat beached. Quickly, I looked around for whoever brought it here. A few feet away stood the man I had seen from the ship. His hat was gone, revealing long braids that had been pulled back. My gaze trailed up his body and I examined his many nautical-themed tattoos. He turned and looked at me with a smile that melted my soul. The sun glimmered in his golden eyes.

"Well, there you are. I was beginning to wonder if the seas were playing tricks on me. It's not every day you see a nude woman with blue hair on a deserted island. Where did you come from?" He slowly stepped closer to me.

My heart pounded in my chest. After what had happened with my uncle, I wasn't sure what to make of the mystery man that now stood in front of me. I opened my mouth to speak, but all that came out was a small squeak.

The man frowned as his eyes fell on the piece of wood in my hand. "Let me help you. Put down the wood, let me take you back to Caldor." His gaze dropped and focused on the piece of kelp wrapped around my thigh. "See over there?" He pointed to the ship. "That's my ship, Pearl of the Southern Sea. We have a medic on board who can take a look at your leg." Looking me back in the eyes, he raised his hands, palms facing me.

He took another step closer, and I stepped back, looking him up and down. He seemed nice, but was this some sort of trick? I raised the wood and pointed it at him.

Stopping his advances, he removed his coat and extended it out to me. "Please let me help you. Take this, cover-up, and I will take you to the mainland. Once there, we can get you help, and try to get you home."

Our eyes locked, and I stared him down. We stood there in silence for some time. My gaze darted from him to the ship then back to him. He seemed as if he really wanted to help me. I couldn't stay here forever, and he may be my only way off this island. Finally, I dropped the makeshift weapon, stepped closer, and took the coat from his hand. Draping it around my shoulders, the weight of it nearly crushed me. I rubbed my hands on the inside of it, taking in its silky texture. Back in Alari, we would never cover ourselves with this much fabric, if anything at all. Often tops would be made from shells and coral, but those were typically for special events or ceremonies.

The man stepped closer, grabbed each side of the jacket's opening, and pulled it closed. "There we go. My crew would have a field day if I brought a naked woman on board. Make sure to keep this closed tight. If I catch any of them looking at you the wrong way, I will throw them overboard to sacrifice them to the Delmari."

"What did you just say?" The words shot out of my mouth before I realized I had spoken. They scraped against my throat as they were forced out. Several coughs escaped my lips to try to clear my throat, but it didn't ease the burn.

The man smirked. "Ah, so you do speak. Very good. One-sided conversations are very awkward. I also have a feeling we have a lot to talk about." He spun me around and wrapped his arm around me, forcing me to walk with him toward the little boat.

Again, I forced out words, this time they came out easier. "What do you mean, *the Delmari*?" I tried to pull away from him.

He held me tighter. "You're on his island. The last time someone was on this island, my grandfather fought a monster to keep Elswyth safe. I am following in his footsteps. Now get in the boat, love. Don't make this harder than it needs to be." He pushed me toward the boat, and I stepped in and sat on the bench. "Good girl. See, that wasn't so hard."

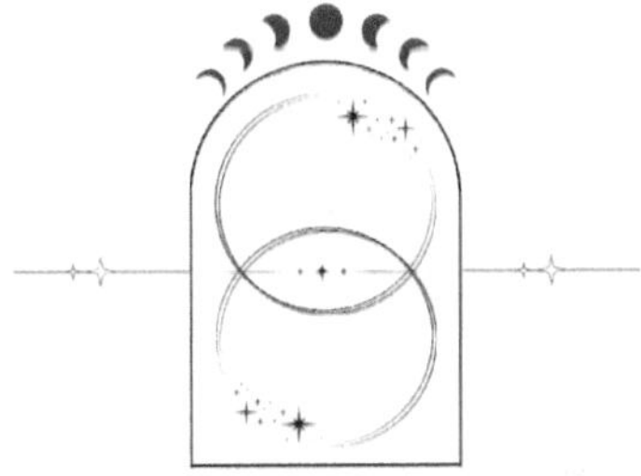

# Five

We rode back to the ship in silence. I cursed myself out in my mind. I told myself I would not be another victim, yet here I was, being forced onto a ship without the one thing I found that could protect me. Once onboard, I could not escape the gaze of the crew. For the first time, I felt anxious about my body. Pulling the jacket tighter, I wished I could jump overboard and swim off into the deep blue to escape them.

"What are you looking at?" My captor boomed. "Get back to work! If I catch any one of ya looking at her again, I will feed you to the Delmari. Understood?" He pulled me in close to him once again, and I breathed in his salty citrus scent. Being close to him brought me comfort. I was happy that he was true to his word that he was going to help me.

Again, he brought up the Delmari and a shiver shot down my spine. What was the thing that he was referring to by my family's name?

"Aye, Captain!" They all responded and returned to their duties.

The captain guided me toward the back of the ship. As we walked, he eyed a tall woman and motioned for her to follow us. He opened a door and pushed me through it. Once they were in behind me, they shut and locked the door. The room was a small office with a long table with a map, a few chairs, a window looking out to the sea, and a staircase leading downward.

"Killian, what the hell is this? When you said you wanted to run ashore, this is not what I thought you meant," the woman sneered.

"After the Delmari attack last night, I thought he would return to where it all began. That is why I wanted to come here. I did not expect to find a naked woman! But, I guarantee you she knows something about the attack!" He snarled.

"She looks frightened! Do you not have any manners? Did you even introduce yourself to her, or did you just abduct her?" When the man said nothing, the woman pushed past him and walked over to me. "Hello. My name is Vari, and this is Killian. I like to call him Captain

Ass Hat." She sent him a pointed glare, then looked back at me with a smile. The sun shone through the window and illuminated her dark-olive skin. "What is your name?"

"She won't answer you. After I got her off the island and into the boat, she refused to speak to me. Hell, I only got her to say one thing, and that was after I brought up the Delmari!"

"My name is Calliope!" I cut him off before he could say anything else. "Tell me about this Delmari. Please." Dread washed over me. I had a feeling I knew exactly who they were talking about. The name had to be no coincidence.

"Sixty years ago, a tentacled creature came from that island, attacked us, and tried to take our land. While the creature was here, it rained for months. Coastal lands flooded. That island used to be a part of a larger archipelago, but those islands are now lost to us," Killian began.

Vari continued for him. "Our grandfather defeated the monster and sent him back to the fathoms below. He returned last night and destroyed many ships."

Tears filled my eyes as they spoke. "I am so sorry. I didn't mean to cause all this destruction."

"So, you did bring back the Delmari!" Killian whipped a blade out from the sheath on his thigh. He pushed forward, and I stepped back until I was up against the table. He continued and held the blade to my neck. "Tell us everything, or I will slice your throat. As Captain of the DarkSea Pirates, I am not afraid to do what is needed to get the answers I seek."

"Killian!" Vari yelled.

He shot her a glare. "That's *captain* to you!" He looked back at me. "Now tell me everything."

I whimpered as he gently pressed the cold steel to my skin. "My full name is Calliope Mariana Delmari, Princess of Alari. I came here in search of my uncle, thinking my mother had done something terrible to him to steal the throne. Unfortunately, I brought him something he needed to complete his plans. I did not mean to. I just want to go home. On that island is a portal that will return me, but my uncle, the Delmari, as you call him, stole my magic. I cannot shift back into my mer form. I am stuck here at the mercy of a pirate who hates me for just being at the wrong place at the wrong time." Sobs rattled from me as I spoke, and my vision blurred from the tears that filled them.

Killian held my stare for a long, silent moment. Slowly, he lowered the blade and took a step back. "I am not the type of man who treats women like this. I apologize." He sheathed his blade and looked toward his sister. "Vari, get her some clothes. We are gonna finish what our grandfather could not." Killian looked back at me with determination in his eyes. "I will get you home, little mermaid, if it is the last thing I do."

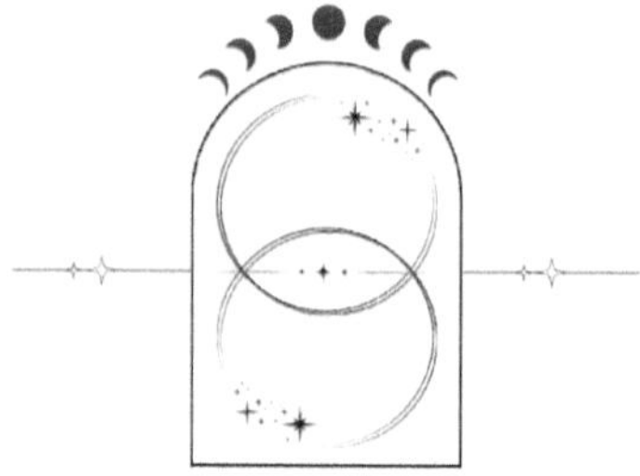

# Six

Vari provided me with a pair of light blue pants that were tight around the ankles and had a long slit down the side that exposed my legs. The top she gave me wrapped around my breasts to cover them, but had no sleeves and stopped right above my belly button. Vari tied the wrap behind me in a beautiful bow. Even though I was not used to wearing clothes, these were light and flowy enough that they did not bother me.

Killian had the medic see me, a woman named Wren. When the kelp wrappings were removed from my leg, I was in shock to see a tattoo that was not there before. It was as if my skin had been cut open and pulled back to reveal the ice-blue scales underneath. A reminder of what I once was, and would never be again.

Killian informed me during the journey, I was to stay in the room below his office, which was his private chamber. Off the side of his room was a small balcony. The top of the banister was gold, and the spindles were black wood that was twisted together. I sat on the floor of it, looking out at the sea for the entire trip to the mainland. My heart ached as I stared off at the dark, sparkling water. How I wished I could jump in, and swim deep into its depth to explore. I stood and clenched the railing so tight the whites of my knuckles showed.

All of my frustrations finally forced their way out of me, and I screamed until the sound formed into words. "I will find you! I will kill you! I will reclaim what is mine!" I repeated the words over and over. Tears streamed down my face and fell into the ocean below. How I hated them for being able to return home.

A firm grip held my shoulder and pulled me back away from the railing. I spun around to Captain Ass Hat, as Vari called him, worry filling his eyes. We stood there for a moment in silence, and then Killian pulled me close to him and gently rubbed my back.

"Shh, little mermaid. He can't hurt you anymore. I made a promise to you, and I intend to keep it. We will get your magic back and return you home," he said in a hushed voice. Releasing me from his embrace, he ushered me back inside. "We will get to shore in about two hours. Why don't you lay down in bed and rest?"

I looked down at the rectangle we stood in front of. Large pieces of cloth were draped over it. Raising my eyebrow, I looked back up to him.

"Have you ever seen a bed before? Let me show you." He pulled back the cloth and laid down. He patted the spot next to him.

Laying down next to Killian, my body sank into it. "Wow, this is really soft."

"What do you sleep in back home?" he asked.

"Giant clam shells. We curl up in them." Now laying in this bed, I was not sure that I could ever return to a clam shell. This was the most comfortable I had ever been. It was so soft and warm, I never wanted to get up.

"Interesting," he said softly. Wrapping his arm around me, he pulled me into him. I took in his salty citrus scent and nuzzled into his chest. Never had I laid with a man before, but with Killian, it felt natural. "I really am sorry about earlier," he continued. "The last time someone was on that island, they brought de-struction to our realm. I should not have assumed that about you." Killian tucked a piece of my hair behind my ear. Heat rose to my cheeks as I stared into his eyes.

"It is ok. If I was in your position, I would have done the same. Maybe even worse if my mother wished it."

"Does your mother often make you do 'worse things'?" Concern grew in his eyes.

Pressing my lips into a firm line, I thought about it for a moment. Everything I believed she was doing to harm the people of Alari was most likely to protect them from Arik. Could the people she had executed have been his accomplices in the nefarious plans he had? Was I so wrong about everything? Was I also wrong about my mother making me use my voice to make people forget?

"Looking back, I think everything she ever did was to protect the people of Alari. All she wanted was for them not to remember Arik. I wonder if the reason she wants them to forget was because of the way he really treated the mer." I pulled my gaze away from him and frowned.

Killian gently lifted my chin so my gaze met with his honeyed eyes. "I never want to see those beautiful blue eyes cry, or those pouty little lips frown ever again." Pulling away his hand, he slowly sat up. Gently, he petted my cheek with the back of his fingers. "I have to get back to the crew. Close your eyes and rest. I will wake you when we get to shore." Killian got out of bed and walked up the stairs.

When he was out of sight, that ache returned to my chest. This time, it wasn't due to my magic being gone.

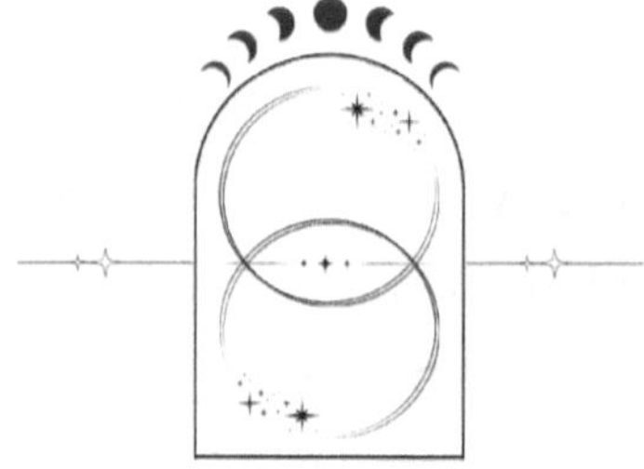

# Seven

All eyes were on me as we walked the gangway to the dock. Part of me wished I had accepted the shoes Vari had offered me, the wood of the dock was rough against my bare feet. But, the shoes were too constricting. I could hear the whispers of the people, all talking about the girl with the blue hair. Apparently, that was not common for the people of Elswyth. Back home, it was not strange to see a rainbow of colors through the the mer. Here it seems that only shades of black, browns, reds, and blondes existed. Killian wrapped his arm around me and pulled me close. When he shot a glare at anyone gawking, they quickly looked away. Many left the docks entirely.

When we were halfway up the pier, a short bald man came rushing toward us. Stopping right before us, he bent down and placed his hands on his knees, breathing heavily. Killian let out a groan.

"Captain Killian, we did not expect you back so soon," the man finally spoke in between his heavy breaths.

"I do not need to report my comings and goings to you. Or have you forgotten?" Killian growled.

Vari came from behind me and stood by my side. She let out a laugh, pointing her nose in the air. "Little Milly thinks he's in charge now?"

"My name is Milton!" He finally straightened his back and caught his breath. "As mayor of Caldor, I am in charge."

Killian released me and took a step forward. "Is that so?" His voice grew so cold it sent a shiver down my spine.

Milton stepped back and stuttered on his words. "It was just that since we did not expect you, we did not have your payment prepared."

"Prepare it. You know where we will be. I expect it by sundown." Killian turned and pointed toward another large ship. The men on this boat were carrying crates of fish to shore. "If not, The Seafarer goes down."

Milton gulped. "You can't. That ship is the most important for our watermen."

Killian turned back to Milton and leaned down so they were at eye level. "Well, then you better figure it out." He straightened his back. "Girls, come along," he chimed.

Vari hooked her arm through mine, and we followed Killian as we walked past Milton. Neither Killian nor Vari spared him a glance.

What type of people did I get myself wrapped up in? I was still so unsure about Killian. He went from being kind, to forcing me on his boat, to holding a knife to my throat, to telling me he would help me return home and care for me. The man I just saw on the dock in Killian's body was not someone I wanted to provoke.

Once off the dock, we stepped onto a stone pathway and walked into town. All eyes were on us. Women and children were ushered inside. Whispers hung in the air. Doors and windows were slammed shut. None of this seemed to bother Killian or Vari, and neither of them said a word as we walked through the streets. I was in awe of the first human town I had ever been in. I wished we walked a little slower so I could take it all in. The only thing I was able to see were buildings made of dark-colored wood. Back home, everything was made from hardened sand and seashells. Some buildings had small flower gardens in front of them. I tried to pull away to reach down to pick one, but Vari tugged on my arm, pulling me away and forcing me to keep moving before I could touch it.

Killian led us up a hill and to a singular structure on the cliffside. It had to be the largest building I had seen since arriving here. It was made from rich brown wood and had a wrap-around porch. I looked out to the ocean, and that ache returned to my chest.

All I craved was to return home, to feel the salt water surround me.

We stopped just a few feet from double doors. Engraved onto the doors were a wave wrapped by a circle. The symbol was one solid line. Killian turned to face me. "Listen to me. Tell no one who you are. If anyone asks you anything, tell them you are with me. Do not say anything to anyone other than that. As a matter of fact, stay with either Vari or me at all times. Got it?"

I nodded in response.

"Good girl," he said with a nod and walked toward the door.

This was the second time he had called me that, and I could not help but blush. I could not help but crave hearing it again from his lips.

Vari leaned closer to me and whispered, "Don't worry. Everything will be just fine. They may seem a little rough, but most of them are good people." She continued walking, pulling me along with her.

Killian opened the double doors and stepped inside. The building was full of people, and I recognized it to be some kind of tavern. Back home, I actually never left the palace grounds until I snuck out to travel here. My mother always wanted to keep me close, she said it was dangerous. I found it to be enthralling, I could not wait to see more of this world above water.

The room smelt strongly of rum and smoke. I coughed several times as I inhaled the scent. There was a bar across the back wall and tables scattered throughout the room. A singular musician played a string instrument on a small stage in the far corner. On the left-hand wall in the back was a staircase leading upstairs.

All eyes turned toward the door and silence hung in the air. But not for long. When the patrons realized who had entered, all mugs rose to the air, and greetings to their captain filled the room.

"Yes, yes, I have returned," Killian teased. "No reason to get too excited." His eyes scanned the room. "Hawk! Van! Upstairs now," he called out.

Two men stood and immediately complied, heading toward the stairs as Killian guided us in the same direction. Once on the second floor, we silently traveled down a long hallway. I loved the feeling of the dark red runner, it was so soft on my bare feet. We entered the room all the way to the end. Despite the intimidating shift in Killian's behavior, I stayed close to him. Vari closed the door behind us once we were all inside. It had a large table in the center of the room with chairs around it. A large window overlooking the ocean. We could see the docks from here. Hawk and Van moved to stand next to the table.

"Take a seat," Killian said, and they did. "We went out to the island earlier, and this is who we found. She is also a victim of the Delmari. It is now the Darksea's top priority to defeat the Delmari and return something it stole from her. Understood?"

"Aye, Captain," they both said in unison.

Killian looked toward me. "Calliope, meet Hawk and Van." He pointed at each one as he said their name. "I trust these two men with my life. They also have ships under my rule."

"Were you able to find out anything else about the beast's location while you were out at sea?" Van asked.

"No," Killian answered in a somber tone. "I also went to the wreckage of The Belle. There were no survivors. Hawk, I want you to coordinate a sailing for Sadie and her crew."

"Aye Captain. I will arrange that for tonight at sundown."

The door behind us opened loudly, causing me to jump out of my skin. I turned and saw an older man walk in. His long white beard was in heavy contrast to his dark skin. He walked with a cane and marched over to Killian.

"You said you were out searching for the Delmari, and you came back with a whore?" The old man yelled. "Your father would be so disappointed! I told him leaving the crew to you would be a mistake! I hate you are proving me right!"

"Adrian!" Vari exclaimed.

Killian's eyes darkened as he looked down at Adrian. "This *whore* was actually found on the Delmari's island. She is the key to finding him and ending him. I do not care you were my father's first mate. I am the captain now. You will not speak that way to me or my crew any longer. Apologize to our guest, or else," he growled.

"How could some girl be the key to finding the monster? You are just making things up to cover your own ass!"

Killian let out a dark laugh and walked over to a bookcase against the wall. He pulled out a book and the shelf slid open to reveal a weapon's cabinet. He reached in and pulled out something that made my jaw drop. "I bet you she is the only one who can wield this thing's magic, and without paying the same price my grandfather did."

Killian walked over to me and forced me to take the silver trident that had been stolen from Alari by my uncle.

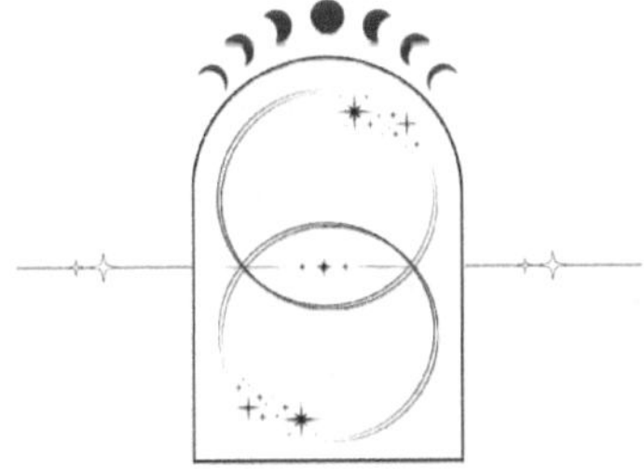

# Eight

Its magic pulsed in my hand and traveled through my body. Tears welled in my eyes. Not from pain, but from the only thing in this world that reminded me of home. The ache in my soul lessened as it was refilled with the magic of Alari. I looked up at Killian and offered a smile. "He's looking for this. He said he would destroy the pirates who took it from him."

"My grandfather was able to steal it and use it against the Delmari in their final battle. Unfortunately, he learned the hard way that magic comes at a price. After he defeated the Delmari, the magic took from his essence to replace what was used during the battle," Killian said.

"Being human, grandfather could not handle what the trident took from him. He passed two days after the battle," Vari continued.

"It was then passed on to my father, and then to me once he passed," Killian added in a somber tone.

Adrian looked at me with anger still in his eyes. "And why do you think the trident will not take from her as it did Caspian?"

"Because I am from the world this comes from," I said plainly.

Adrian's face dropped to a blank expression. All he could do was stare and blink at me. Silence hung in the air for a few moments. "That means you are..." Adrian finally spoke but trailed off.

"A mermaid. Yes. I was before he stole my powers. Now I am nothing more than a human. The only reminder I have is this." I pulled the cloth away from my thigh and revealed the tattooed scales.

"I..." Adrian began, then paused. "I am sorry," he said softly.

I nodded in response, then examined the trident. Gently, I ran my fingers across the cold metal, finding the indent where the Gem once laid. We had to get it back and return it home.

Vari was next to her brother and whispered something in his ear, too quiet for me to make out.

Killian's response was loud enough for me to hear. "It belongs to her. We all have the same goals. I know we can trust her with it. You worry too much, Vari."

I stepped closer to them. "You can trust me. I promise you that. However, this is my first time seeing the trident in person. I am not even sure of the magic it wields. Arik stole it from us all those years ago."

"Who is Arik?" Van asked.

"Arik is the monster we are after. Delmari is our family name." The words slipped out of my mouth before I could stop them. My chest tightened as anxiety crept in. I prayed to The Mother that they wouldn't react poorly to that tidbit of information.

"Our?" Adrian's eyes narrowed.

"Yes. Arik is my uncle. I did not know him prior to meeting him yesterday. I wish I never did. I wish I just stayed in Alari."

Killian walked over to me, gently taking the trident from my hands. "Then you wouldn't have met me. And I promise you all of this will be worth it in the end for that alone," he laughed. "I am going to put this away for now." He walked back over to the weapon's case, put it back, and moved the bookshelf to hide it once again.

"Excuse me, Captain," someone said from the doorway. All eyes quickly turned toward the voice. A tall man stood there. "Sorry to interrupt. Baldy is here. He says he's got something for you."

A smile grew on Killian's face. "Send him up. Hawk, you have your orders. Van, I want you to make sure all ships are seaworthy." He turned his honeyed eyes to me and smiled. "Vari, will you take her up to my room and let her rest and bathe?"

"Aye!" Everyone responded.

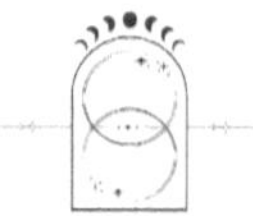

Vari led me down the hall and up another flight of stairs to a large apartment. Vari quickly gave me a tour. It had a sitting area and a kitchen in the entry room, and in the back was a bedroom with a wall of glass that overlooked the sea. Once in the bathing room, she gave me short instructions on what everything was and how plumbing worked. Humans require so many different solutions to keep themselves clean. In Alari, we used natural mud to nourish our skin, scales, and hair. Then we would allow the ocean to wash it away to keep us clean. I stared up at the running water for a long moment. Never in my entire life had I heard of anything called a shower. Before she left the bath chamber, she told me this was going to be one of the best experiences as a human I would ever experience.

Stepping in, I allowed the hot water to run down my body. Once it did, all the tension I did not realize I was holding was released. A soft moan escaped my lips. There was nothing I loved more than the sensation of water on my skin. I put two pumps of something called shampoo into my hand. The scent of mint and citrus filled my nose. Slowly, I worked the shampoo into my long hair, focusing on the scalp. Once that was thoroughly applied I rinsed it out and applied a deep conditioner. Vari told me it was best if I let it sit on my hair for a few moments before rinsing it out.

As I waited, I allowed the water to wash over my body. Vari was right. This was a magical experience. Where did this steady supply of water come from and why did it lack salt? Still, I had not fully gotten used to my legs. After all the walking and standing today, they had grown tired. The floor of the shower was slightly slippery, and I really had to be careful, or I could easily slip.

After a while, I heard a soft knock on the door.

"Just checking to make sure you are doing alright," Vari called out from behind the door.

"Everything is fine. You were right! This does feel amazing," I responded.

She chuckled before she answered. "See, being human isn't all bad. I will be just out here if you need anything."

"Thank you."

No, being human wasn't all bad so far... for someone who was used to it. But, for me, all I wanted was my fin and to dive into the depths of the ocean. There was truly a lack of a place to soak, I craved the feeling of being fully submerged in water. I wanted to return home. While the view of the sea here was beautiful, and the people were interesting, my heart belonged in Alari.

I belonged in Alari.

I ran the water through my hair to remove the conditioner, washed my human body, and exited the shower. Wrapping the large fluffy towel around me, I walked over to the mirror. Steam coated the shiny surface, and I wiped it away to be able to stare at myself. I had the same face, and the same blue hair, but I was missing the gills that were on my neck. Slowly, I ran my fingers down the smooth skin that was now there. Before I knew it, tears filled my eyes, and I let out a sob. Everything I had been holding in finally forced its way out. No longer able to hold myself up on my exhausted human legs, I fell to the floor, rolled onto my side, and pulled my knees to my chest.

The door busted open, and Vari rushed inside. Without a word, she sat me up and wrapped me in a tight hug. We sat there in silence for some time as she gently rubbed my back. Slowly, my sobs turned to soft sniffles.

I raised my gaze to meet hers, and she offered me a warm smile.

"I cannot imagine what you are going through, or how you are feeling," she said in nearly a whisper. "I promise you that my brother and I will make sure we get you home. We will take care of you until then."

"Thank you," I whimpered. "It means a lot."

Her face grew somber. "I know what it is like to have a man take away something from you. Do not let what happened define you. You are strong. You are brave. You will get your vengeance on him."

My eyes grew wide as I realized what she meant. "Did you?"

"Damn right, I did. My brother and I hunted him down all the way to the isle of Varia in the north. He won't be hurting anyone else. Can't when your weapon was removed." A smirk grew on her face. "He thought I showed him mercy when I spared his life. But it was not mercy I gave. For the rest of his days, he will live knowing what it is like to have your body violated, to have your choice taken. I hope when he is offered a drink from a bar patron, panic rattles his bones. When he wakes in the middle of the night, I hope he fears what lurks in the shadows. Since then, I have opened the crew to all women who are in search of finding a place safe from those who wish to harm us, and to teach them the true strength we all carry within our hearts."

Turning to her, I wrapped her in a hug. We sat there for some time in each other's embrace. Physical affection was not something that I was used to, but I found it extremely comforting. After a while, she stood and extended her hand out to me. "Let's get you dressed and get you something to eat."

I took her hand and stood. "That sounds wonderful. I am starving."

"What do mermaids eat, anyway?" She asked with a raised brow.

"Fish," I responded plainly.

"Oh! You are going to love this town then. Down the street, there is a restaurant that serves the best seafood you will ever have! You have to get this pasta dish with lobster, scallops, shrimp, and muscles!"

"What is pasta?"

"Oh, this is going to be so much fun!" She squealed. Vari pulled me into the bedroom where my clothes had already been laid out on the bed. "Hurry and get dressed! I am going to take you around town and show you how humans live!"

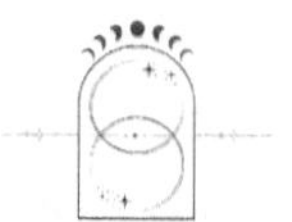

That night, we all stood on the beach. Small wooden boats lined the shore. The sky was clear, and the moon's light reflected off the ocean. The crew from the ship and patrons from the tavern were all in attendance, as well as some faces I did not recognize. Everyone wore black, and since I literally had nothing, Vari let me borrow a little black dress that hugged my curves.

This ritual had always been performed after a pirate had lost their life. According to them, sailing was a way to release souls from this world and pass on to the next.

Killian stepped forward and turned to face the crowd, clearing his throat before he spoke. "The Delmari has returned. Last night, one of our ships was just off the harbor when many of us witnessed the brutal attack by the beast. This morning, I took a crew out to the wreckage. Unfortunately, the crew of The Ocean's Belle did not survive the attack. Sadie was a wonderful second mate and will be missed, as will all the people who we lost."

He listed off every name of who perished. As he did, one of the small boats was pushed out to sea. Once all names were said, archers stepped forward and loaded their bows with arrows tipped with fire. They shot the watercrafts, and when arrows landed, each vessel went up in flames. Everyone around me stood in silence. Some of the women were on their knees, sobbing into their hands. Vari and Killian both had somber expressions, and tears streamed down their cheeks. Their eyes locked onto me, and they slowly walked over. Killian pulled me close to him and looked out toward the ocean. It took only a few minutes for each of them to be lit. The burning boats all drifted off to sea, and we all watched in silence as they traveled farther and farther. I could not help to think of the traditions of Alari when we had souls pass on. There was a sacred trench south of the castle. The bottom of which is a volcano. We would send the bodies of the deceased down the trench to return. Tears welled in my eyes, and I wiped them away. One by one, the flames extinguished as the burning vessels sank.

Before the last one could sink, dark clouds formed quickly, hiding the moon and stars. Lightning flashed across the sky and thunder boomed. I cowered from the sound. Never had I heard anything like it. Not even a second later, the sky opened up, heavy rain poured, and the final flame was finally extinguished. Killian rushed over to me with a worried expression. "Hurry back to the tavern. We need to get to high ground now. We are in our dry season. It is not due to rain for another month."

Vari took my hand and squeezed. "Hopefully this is just some freak storm, and not one brought on by the Delmari."

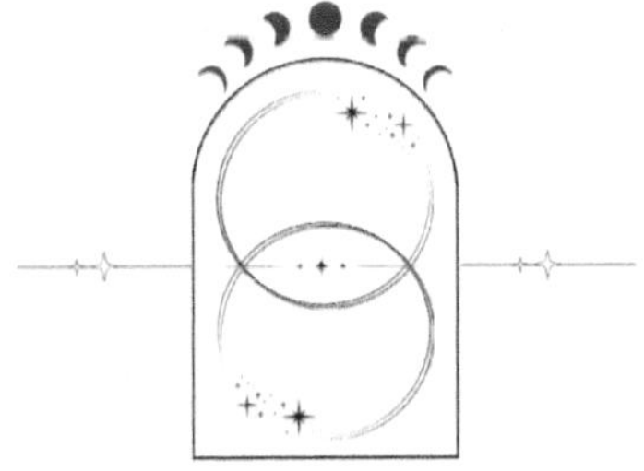

# Nine

Three days had passed, and the heavy rains continued. The beaches no longer existed, and the water was nearly up to the first building of the town. Killian opened the tavern to those who lived close to the water so they could escape the flooding. Any boat that attempted to sail out was attacked by Arik. He only returned early in the morning for fresh clothes. Never had he slept in here, so I wasn't sure exactly what he was doing throughout the day and night. He claimed it was important for me to stay hidden. According to him, it was important not to let Arik know I was here.

Vari had brought me some books about the land of Elswyth. I learned of fae attacks to the west, which I had assumed to be the cursed fae of Orilon. My mother had talked about that poor realm once or twice. While we did not visit the other realms, we did often receive written communication from them, all except Tarak.

I was getting antsy. Sitting in here all day was driving me mad. We needed to do something, hiding here would not stop my uncle. I stayed up all night, waiting for Killian to return to his room. Once he had, I locked the door and blocked his path from leaving so he could not rush away again.

"Killian, I want to help. I cannot just stay locked in here all day with nothing to do but wait! It is driving me crazy!"

He turned to me and sighed, and it was then I noticed how dark bags had settled under his eyes. "I need to keep you safe until it is time to strike. You cannot leave this room until then."

"When will be the time, then? And what is the plan? I have no idea how to even wield the trident! I am not even sure I could!"

He stepped closer to me, so quickly that I staggered back. My back was now pressed against the wood of the door. He placed one hand above me to cage me in, and the other gently lifted my chin. Breath caught in my throat as he looked down at me with a placating expression. "Oh, my little mermaid. I am trying to get it all figured out for you. I promise. Please, just give me one more day."

"Give me the trident. That way I can at least begin to attune myself to its magic."

Killian smirked at me, released my chin, and booped the top of my nose. "You are so bossy. It's cute, but no."

"No?! You said you trusted me!"

"I do. But we cannot risk the chance that if it is out, your uncle may be able to find it."

"Killian, I will not ask again. Give it to me, now."

"Make me." He leaned in closer so his face was just an inch from mine.

The air electrified around us as the thunder boomed. My entire body tingled as his hand dropped from my chin and his fingertips gently grazed down my arm. Heat flooded my cheeks.

"Killian..." I breathed. "What are you doing?"

"Shh, little mermaid. I need to blow off some steam, and I am sure you want to explore your new human body. Am I right? You want to know why heat is building in between your legs right now, don't you? Let us help each other out, then I will give you the trident. Deal?"

I squirmed a bit. How did he know the feeling I had? It wasn't just heat that built. It was an ache. I gave a small nod.

A low growl escaped his throat and hunger grew in his eyes. "Oh no, love. I want to hear you say yes. I will not touch you until I have your full consent. Will you let me explore in between those sexy thighs of yours?"

"Please," I whimpered. My core ached for him. Never once had I experienced the touch of a man, but I craved Killian.

"Good girl," he breathed. His hand slipped down in between my legs and gently rubbed the apex of my thighs.

I cursed myself for the pants I was wearing. His fingers rubbed harder, and I let out a small moan.

"That is music to my ears, Calliope," he said just before he pressed his lips to mine.

The kiss was much gentler than I imagined it would be. Just looking at him, you would never expect the pirate captain to be a gentle lover. He pulled his soft lips away from mine. His citrus and salt scent filled my nose, and I kissed him back, increasing the passion between us. I could feel him harden against me. My heartbeat quickened as I slowly reached to touch it.

Quickly, he pulled away. "Such an eager one you are. Strip for me," he demanded. I did just as he asked. Killian took my hand and guided me to stand in front of the full-length mirror that was mounted on the wall and stood behind me. "Gods, you have the most beautiful body I have ever seen. Sit."

I did as he said, and he sat behind me, positioning me in between his legs. "What are you doing?" I asked.

"Don't ask questions. Spread your legs for me."

His commanding voice made my knees weak. Doing as I was told, he smirked. His hands found their way to my breasts, and he rubbed them. As he slid my nipples between two fingers and pulled, a gasp of pleasure escaped my throat. Staring at myself in the mirror, my gaze fell from where his hands were making me forget how to breathe to the little wet slit in between my legs.

Killian's gaze followed mine. "Oh, curious about that, are we?" His hands traveled down my body and gently brushed against the outside of my most intimate part. Too slowly, his fingers ran up and down it. "You are so wet for me." He pulled his fingers away and put them in front of my face. They glistened with my juices. "Lick it and tell me how you taste."

Slowly, I dragged my tongue up his fingers, tasting myself. "Sweet."

He lowered his hand and pushed two fingers inside my entrance. He quickly pulled it out and brought it to his own lips. A huge smile grew on his face as he groaned in delight. I watched him as he sucked on his fingers. "I had to taste for myself. You're right. You are delicious." He lowered his hand once again and slid his fingers inside of me. Slowly, he thrusted them in and out.

I let out a moan as he played with me. "Please, harder," I demanded.

"Beg, and maybe I will." The temptation in his voice only made me want him more.

"Killian please," I begged. "I need more."

He continued, increasing the force. My body filled with pleasure, but it ended all too quickly. He pulled his fingers away, stood, walked over to the front of me, and forced me to look up at him.

"I am sure you are curious about what a male body looks like." He removed his shirt, then slowly removed his pants. His considerable length sprung into my face. My eyes crossed as I focused on it. "Like what you see, love?"

"That is huge," I whimpered.

Killian chuckled. "Wrap those beautiful pouty lips around it."

I got onto my knees and looked up at him. Breath caught in my throat as I examined his full length. Nervously, I wrapped my lips around its tip and sucked gently on it. Killian threw back his head and let out a groan. His fingers ran through my hair and stopped as his hand reached the back of my head. Pushing just a little, he made me take more of him into my mouth. My eyes went wide as he slid deeper inside me. Once half of his length was in, he stopped pushing on my head to allow me to adjust to him. I swirled my tongue around as I continued to suck on him. After a moment, he pulled away, and a strand of spit connected me to the tip of his cock.

"Don't move," he commanded. Walking behind me, he sat on the ground once again. He grabbed my hips and pulled me back, causing me to mount him. He lined himself up with my entrance but did not enter me. One of his hands grabbed me by my cheeks and forced me to look into the mirror. "Watch how I fuck you, Calliope." Slowly, he lowered me onto him. I let out a moan as the head fully slipped in. My body opened up to take his full girth. "Gods, you are perfect."

Killian thrusted upward to make me take more of him. A moan escaped my lips as more of him entered me. Through the reflection, I watched as his length disappeared. The feeling was overwhelming as he stretched me beyond what I ever imagined. I begged him for more, and he obliged. It was not long before the full length of him was deep inside me. Looking into the mirror, I watched him slide in and out of me. My body was overcome with pleasure I never experienced.

A pleasure that I could easily become addicted to.

"Don't stop please." I could not describe the feeling building inside me. It was beyond pure euphoria. Quivering against him, I was about to explode from the pleasure.

Killian stopped thrusting and nearly pulled out all the way. "Oh no, you are not allowed to come yet, love.

Fuck yourself, and maybe, just maybe, I will give you the privilege of coming on my cock."

"No, please, don't stop," I pleaded. "I need you deep inside me." Nervousness took over. If I were to be in charge of my own movements, would I be able to please the man who brought so much pleasure to me? Would I continue to feel that pleasure?

"If you want it, take it." He leaned back and rested on his elbows. Looking back at him, I slowly bounced on him. "Good girl. You take me so well. Don't stop until I say so."

I bounced harder and faster on him until I had him slamming on my innermost wall. The moans that escaped my lips got louder with each bounce. I could not believe I was doing this, I loved this, or that I craved this. Back home, I never imagined such carnal pleasures.

Killian grabbed hold of my hips and started thrusting again, harder and faster than before. The pleasure was overwhelming just before he exploded inside of me, and stars filled my vision. He continued to fuck me until I felt his cock twitch.

Quickly, he sat up and pulled out of me. He spun me around and sat me back on the ground. Getting on his knees, he stroked himself until his tip shot out his essence, and it covered my chest.

A satisfying ache filled my body and I smiled up at him in a daze. This man was a god. He had to be to provide such overwhelming pleasure.

"If I thought you were beautiful before, I cannot deny you are even more stunning with my cum all over your chest." He smirked and stood. Offering his hand to me, he assisted me up. "Let's get us cleaned up, then we can go train with the trident."

"Will you join me in the shower?" I asked with a smile.

Killian's honey-colored eyes lit up. "Absolutely."

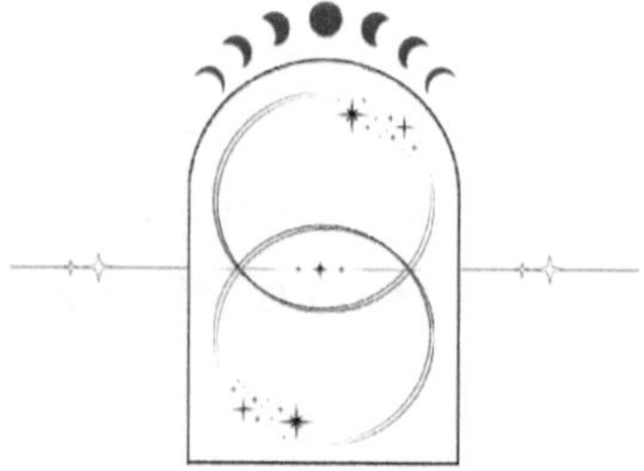

# Ten

Heavy rain continued to fall, soaking both Killian and me to the bone. We were just outside of town, out of the view of the sea and away from prying eyes. Gripping the trident tight with both hands, its magic pulsed through me. For the last hour, I tried to connect myself further with it. Even though my magic was gone, I tried to call forth a kernel of it to see if it would combine with the magic of the trident. With all the stories I had been told of the trident, it was our family's most powerful weapon. It was gifted to the first mer king and my ancestor by The Mother and her daughter Nera. Was it anything without the Gem of Alari? Even without the Gem, I could still feel its power. What exactly could the trident do without it?

For over an hour, Killian watched me as I acted out using the trident in battle. Thrusting it forward, I pretended to stab my imaginary foe. Quickly, I spun and mimicked the movement as if someone was attacking me from behind. He shook his head and let out a chuckle under his breath. "Love, if that is how you fight, I don't think we have any hope of defeating your uncle."

I shot him a pointed glare. "I am doing my best!" Marching over to him, red filled my vision. "I am in a new world, dealing with a new body, and without the comfort of my magic to guide me. The trident had not been in Alari for at least thirty years before I was born! My mother never even talked about it or its capabilities. I have no idea what I am doing."

He pushed off the tree he was leaning against and took a step to close the gap between us. Rain ran down and dripped off his chiseled face. "Calliope. I am sorry. I didn't mean anything by it. It was a joke."

"The joke wasn't funny!" I shouted at him.

Killian let out a deep breath. "May I show you what my father taught me?" he asked in a soft voice.

I glared at him for a moment before nodding and handing over the trident.

Killian took it from my hands and stepped into the clearing, going over all the stances and positions he was taught. The silver glimmered in his hands, and Killian's eyes glowed as he wielded the weapon. It was then that it clicked for me. The trident was no longer just a Delmari family heirloom. Three generations of the Darksea line had guarded the trident from the monster my uncle had become. Though this land seemed to be one of no magic, could it be possible that the Darkseas created their own to protect the trident? And in doing so, change it from being responsive to a Delmari heir?

"Killian?" I spoke softly, but not weakly.

"Yes?" He stopped mid-movement and looked down at me.

"What do you feel when you wield the trident?"

He turned to face me, with his head slightly cocked and an eyebrow raised. "What do I feel?"

I nodded and walked over to him. I placed my hands on top of his. "Close your eyes. Focus on the Trident."

Killian closed his eyes and took slow and even breaths. "I am not sure how to describe what I feel."

"Try."

He stayed silent for a long while. The rain poured down on us. "Like it is flowing through me and becoming one with my soul."

A smile grew across my face. "Killian. The trident is not mine to wield. It is yours. It has attuned to you."

He opened his eyes and looked down at me with a look of shock. "Impossible. I know nothing of magic."

I shook my head as a smile spread across my face. "It doesn't matter. It chose you. When your family became the caretakers of the weapon, your soul mixed with it."

Killian stepped back, pulling away from me. "Give me some space. I want to try something."

I obliged, creating more distance between us.

Killian raised the trident into the air. "I am Killian Darksea," he boomed. "Captain of the Darksea pirates, protector of the Southern Sea. Hear me, Tempuno." He spoke directly to the god of storms. Silence fell in the air for a moment, and then three bolts of lightning flashed across the sky, followed by a loud roll of thunder. "Hear me, Calypso." He now called out the god of the seas. "Here me, Nera." When he spoke to the mother of the mer, my heart pounded in my chest. She was the goddess that I had the closest relationship with. I prayed she would help us above all others. "Grant me strength and guidance, for tomorrow, I will take a small crew back to the Delmari's island. Grant us safe passage. Allow us to end the storm that threatens the balance of this world. Allow the little mermaid to restore her magic, and return to the sea she calls home. For if you grant us this, I will dedicate my life in your honor."

Killian stared up at the sky. The only sound was the rain growing heavier. Killian did not falter. He stayed there with the trident raised to the sky. After another moment of silence, a bolt of lightning struck the trident on its head. Electricity buzzed around the prongs. Killian lowered it so it was at eye level with him.

"Thank you," he said softly. "I will not disappoint you."

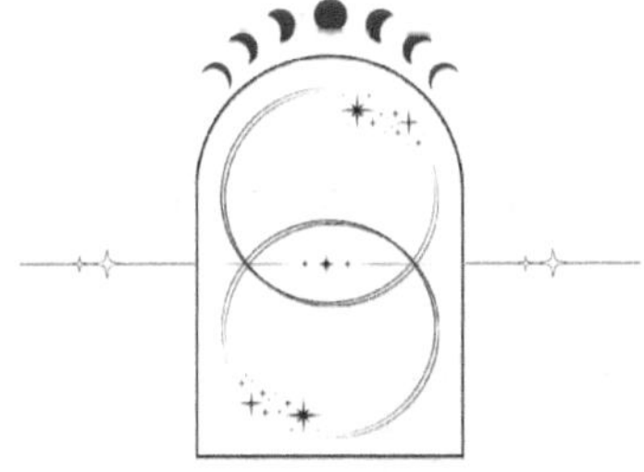

# Eleven

Three more days passed, and still the rain did not let up. The sea level had now risen to the point it was flooding people's homes near the shore. Early that morning, Killian gathered a small crew, and we boarded a ship, sailing off to return to where it all began. Anxiety filled me to my core as we walked toward the dock. I was not sure if I was ready to face my uncle, but it was now or never.

When we got to the seashore, most of the boats that had been docked were missing, and some were adrift out in the harbor. Killian's ship, The Dark Seafarer, was still docked. Lucky for all of us, this was a floating dock. If it was built into the ground, we would have been out of luck.

Quickly, we all made our way down and onboard the ship. After about a half hour, we were ready to sail. Killian instructed me to stay in his office. That way, I would be out of the way of the crew until we got to our destination. The sway of the boat from the massive waves had a knot growing in my stomach. It was as if at any moment I was going to release the contents of it.

After a short amount of time, Vari entered the office. A puddle of water formed under her feet as she leaned against the door for support. "I wanted to bring you this," she said as she extended her arm and held out a small pouch.

"What is that?" I questioned as I slowly walked over to her, swaying with each step.

"Ginger candy. I know if I am feeling sick, you must be. I know you lived in the sea and all, but being aboard a ship during a storm is a whole nother beast. These help, a little," she said with a smile.

I took the pouch from her, removed a piece of candy, and popped it in my mouth. The spiced taste caused me to scrunch my face.

"I know they taste horrible, but it's totally worth it. Please keep the whole bag. You will need it."

"Vari!" I heard Killian call from beyond the door. "I need you at the helm."

"I have to go, but I will check on you again if I can."

Before I could respond, she had gone out the door. In the short amount of time I had known her, Vari had become a good friend. As much as I hated to admit it, so had Killian. Truly, I was going to miss both of them when I returned home. Hopefully, mother was not too mad at me for running away, and would allow me to visit. That was if I was ever allowed to leave the castle again.

The sound of splintering wood pulled me from my thoughts of home. The ship rocked with such force that I fell on my ass. Screams could be heard from the out-side. I forced myself up and rushed over to the door, pulling it open. My mouth fell agape at what I saw. Large red tentacles arose from the surface of the sea and waved in the air. They towered over the ship.

"Abandon ship!" a man called out.

"I am not getting into the water with that beast!" another said.

"It doesn't matter if you go in the water, or stay aboard. We are all dead!" a third answered.

A tentacle smashed down on the ship again, and my body slammed into the door frame from the force. A tentacle swept across the deck, knocking several of the crew into the water. It slammed into the mast, breaking the solid wood. The loud cracking sound overwhelmed my ears. It wrapped around the pole and threw the mast into the ocean.

"Calliope!" Killian called out.

"I am here!" I responded.

He jumped down from the deck above with the trident in hand. When his eyes landed on me, they went wide with worry. Quickly, he rushed over to me and wrapped me in his arms. "Don't worry, love. I am going to get us out of this safe."

"Wh-where is Vari?" I asked, holding on to Killian for support.

"She is getting the lifeboats ready!" He looked around at the remainder of his scrambling crew. "Everyone to the lifeboats now!" On his last word, another tentacle rose and slammed down onto the ship, breaking through it. The ship rocked back from the impact. Screams filled the air. Killian threw me over his shoulder. He held me tight with one arm, the other gripped the trident. "Here goes nothing," he said under his breath. He pointed the trident toward the tentacle, and when nothing happened, Killian let out a growl.

Another tentacle arose from the water behind him and shot toward us.

"Killian, behind you!" I screamed.

Quickly, he spun us around and stabbed the trident directly into the assaulting tentacle. Bright blue electricity shot through it. The tentacle pulled back from us before it convulsed and fell into the ocean.

"That is what I am talking about!" Killian cheered.

Another tentacle came our way, and again Killian struck it with the trident, whose prongs buzzed with electric power. This time, all the tentacles wrapped around the ship retreated into the dark water. I released the breath I had been holding.

"Don't count this as over yet." Killian placed me back on my feet. Taking my hand, he rushed us to the side of the ship where three small boats floated below us. Two were already full with the remaining crew, and the last boat only carried Vari. Killian ushered me down the rope ladder to get on the small lifeboat. While working our way down, the ship was taking on too much water. Between that and the damage from Arik, the stress on the wood was too much, and it snapped in half. The front nose dived into the water. Once the bow was submerged, it slowly sank. The aft tilted, causing Killian to stagger. Once he steadied himself, he quickly descended the ladder. Before he got halfway down, he jumped onto our small lifeboat, causing it to rock so hard that Vari nearly fell overboard.

"Quickly, get to shore!" Killian called out. He pointed over to the town, which seemed so far away. How long would it take us to reach shore? Would we be able to do so safely?

Vari pulled two paddles out from under the seats. She gave one to Killian. "The two of us will row. Calliope you sit there." She pointed to the bench behind me. The two of them sat on the one across from me and rowed.

"I can help, you know!" I said.

"Oh, love, I am sure you could, but this will be a long trip," Killian responded.

"And, no offense, but with those little noodle arms, we would not make it far," Vari let out a laugh.

"Hey! I can't help my thin arms."

"How about this, love?" He extended the trident out to me. "Hold on to this like your life depends on it."

"May I remind both of you it does?" Vari retorted.

The sea grew eerily silent as we rowed our way back to shore. The only sounds were the rain hitting the surface, and the paddles pushing the water. Even the choppy waves calmed. After about an hour, we seemed no closer to shore. Both Vari and Killian struggled more and more with each row, but they continued to refuse my help. The other two boats were now a good bit ahead. Each had at least four people rowing at a time.

I looked up at the sky, and let the rain wash away the tears that had been flowing down my face. Again, lives had been lost because of me. If I never traveled to this land, Arik would have never gotten the power he need-ed. His tentacles had grown so much since I had last seen him, and I feared how much power he had gained from the Gem. The sound of bubbling water filled the space around me. When I looked down, it was as if the sea was boiling.

"Vari, give it all you got!" Killian called out. The two of them started to row faster.

But it was no use. A red tentacle shot from the water. Before anyone could react, it wrapped around Vari and pulled her under. She did not even have a chance to scream before she was claimed by the sea. Her paddle floated to the surface and bobbed against the waves.

"Vari!" I called out. I leaned over the side to look down, but I could not see anything in the dark ocean.

Killian let out a scream as he ripped the trident from my hands. "Give me back my sister, you beast!" On that last word, he dove into the bubbling ocean.

I reached out for him, trying to get him to stop. But he, too, vanished into the water. Now alone, in the small lifeboat, I contemplated my next move. Before I could decide, I heard a gasp from behind me. I spun to see Killian's head emerging from the sea.

"It is too dark! I can't see anything. He took her! I can't let him keep her," he sobbed. "I promised my father I would protect her. I can't fail him again." He dove under once again.

And again.

And again.

Each time it felt like an eternity before his head broke the surface. All I could do was helplessly watch. My body would not allow myself to jump into the water to help him.

After the fifth time, he climbed back into the lifeboat with his head hung. He took both paddles in hand and began to row. I sat by his side, and he leaned against me. Taking one of the paddles from him, I helped him row us back to shore.

We went the entire way in utter silence.

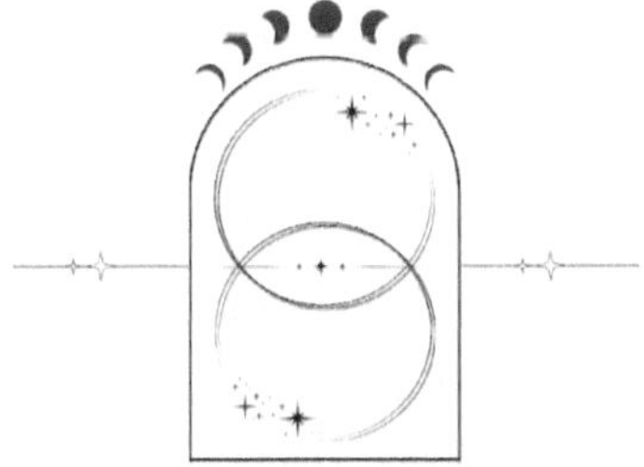

# Twelve

Killian did not get out of bed for three days. I moved to a room downstairs to give him privacy. Every day Hawk, Van, and I tried to enter his room to check on him. The door would be locked, and he would not respond to us. Without Vari, the tavern felt so empty. I missed her laugh and her smile. We all did. With the rain still somehow growing harder, it was impossible to give the lost souls a sailing. Not being able to perform the rite lowered the morale of the entire Darksea crew even more.

Without completing the sailing, the Darkseas believed the souls of the lost were trapped here.

With the rain continuing to get worse, most of Caldor had flooded. The cliff kept us dry, but it would not be much longer until the tavern, too, was underwater. Many of the town's citizens have traveled north to the capital of Elswyth. Though there were mountains to the west, no one traveled that way. No one wanted to face the monstrous beasts who would tear you limb from limb and feast on your flesh beyond the mountains.

One night, I was jolted awake by a familiar sound. This had to be a trick of the mind. Jumping out of bed, I quickly dressed and marched out of the tavern. It was a dangerous game I was playing by leaving without telling a soul. If this was a trap, I was falling right into it, but I had to take the chance. The sound continued to ring in my ears. As I got closer to the waterline, it got louder. The song of the mer called to me. A sweet melody of welcoming and acceptance.

There was no denying what I heard.

These mer sang for me. They knew my name. They called for me. Tears filled my eyes. Could they be from home? Could this be the rescue I craved?

I boarded one of the small lifeboats and paddled as fast as I could toward the sound. The rough seas made it difficult to row forward, but I refused to stop. Praying Arik would not sense my presence, I hoped I would reach who called to me in time.

The wind picked up, and the waves worsened, and I could feel every ebb and flow of the ocean beneath me.

With each wave. I rose and crashed hard as it passed. Still, the song continued.

*Calliope.*

*Calliope.*

*Calliope.*

*Princess of Alari.*

They called my name.

Until they didn't. The only sounds now were of the hard rain and the violent ocean. I turned to see how far I ventured offshore. The town was now on the distant horizon.

"I am here!" I screamed out into the vast ocean. "I am here. Please, take me home," I sobbed.

There was no answer. Was the song something I imagined? Something I had conjured just to make me feel close to home?

The waves continued to grow in size, and I grabbed my paddles tight and fought against them to turn back to shore. A large wave was coming directly my way. There was no way this small boat could make it over. No, this could not be it for me. I paddled harder, hoping I could make it past.

Why did I allow the phantom voices to call me so far from shore? Out of anyone, I should have known how dangerous the lure of the voice could be.

The wave finally met my boat and caused it to capsize, throwing me into the dark sea. I spun in the water from the force, and it was impossible to get my bearings. I tried to kick my feet to swim, but I made no progress getting closer to the surface. On instinct, I opened my mouth, but my human lungs were not made to take in water. The waves continued to beat against my body, and would not allow my head to break the surface. My head felt light, and my eyes fluttered.

I swore arms grabbed me just before everything faded to black.

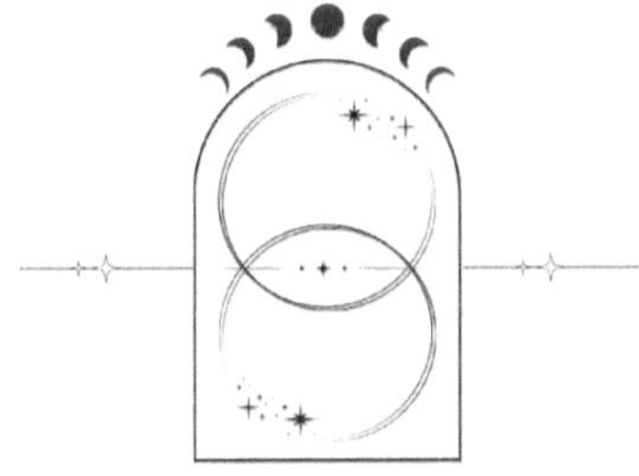

# Thirteen

"Is it really her?" a gentleman's voice asked.

I tried to open my eyes, but they refused to cooperate. The voice sounded so far away... as if it was in another realm... as if this was a dream.

"She answered a call only meant for the Princess of Alari, did she not? It has to be," a woman answered.

"Do you think she will wake soon?"

Again, I tried to open my eyes. The voices started to fade as if they were getting farther and farther from reality.

"In her human body, it is hard to tell," the woman responded.

The two continued to speak, but I was unable to understand them. The harder I tried to make out what

they were saying, the more the words softened until
there was just silence.

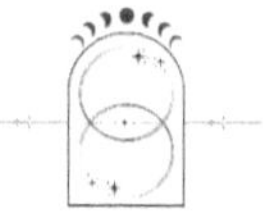

My eyes shot open, and I quickly sat up. Wooziness
filled me at the sudden motion. As my vision came into
focus, I saw an older woman sitting at the edge of the
bed. Her white hair was pulled up into a tight bun atop
her head, and her light blue eyes nearly glowed.

"Easy there. Don't hurt yourself. You are safe."

It was the woman I had heard in my dream.

"Where..." My throat was so dry and hoarse, it was
hard to get words out. "Where am I?" I finally forced out.

The woman stood and walked over to the table next
to the bedside, where she picked up the glass of water
and extended it to me. "Please drink."

I took the cup from her hand and brought it to my lips.
At first, I struggled to swallow, but the more I drank, the
easier it became.

"Good, we will get you more in a moment. My name is
Nera. You are in my home. My children pulled you from
the ocean."

My eyes went wide in recognition. "Nera..."

She let out a chuckle. "So you have heard of me? I was wondering if the people of Alari had forgotten the old ways after all this time. Do not fret, for I have not forgotten you. I would not forget any of my children."

I could not believe my ears. Was I truly in front of the woman where all mer originated? According to legend, Nera was one of The Mother's children. It was she who created the mer and granted us our gifts. We called her the mother of the mer. "Thank you for saving me." That was all I could force myself to say.

"No need to thank me, my dear, for I would save all my children. Pulling you from the Southern Sea was not the only way you needed saving. There is another way you need to be saved, correct?"

I nodded.

"Come with me, child. for I can return to you what was stolen." She turned and walked toward the door.

I jumped out of bed and followed her. As we exited the room, we came out to a small landing in a circular room. Along the wall was a silver spiral staircase leading to more landings and doors. Walking over to the railing, I looked down and my stomach flipped. We were very high up. The entire space was only the stairs that hugged the wall and all the doors.

"Come along," Nera called out. She had already begun to descend the stairs.

I rushed to catch up to her. There were a few others on the stairs, and they bowed as we passed them. Once at the bottom, she opened the door and rushed me outside. The sun hit my face, and I embraced its warmth on my skin. Off in the distance, dark storm clouds loomed in the sky. Nera placed a gentle hand on my shoulder, and I turned to meet her gaze.

"Do not worry. He cannot reach you here. Only those I allow are welcome here. Neither he nor his storm are welcome."

I turned and offered her a warm smile, and she gave me one in response. Releasing me, she continued to walk forward. Before I followed her, I turned to look at the building we exited. It was a very tall lighthouse. The color of it matched my tail exactly, even down to the silver sparkles.

"Come along now so you don't get lost!" she called out to me. I turned toward her and followed. The sandy shore turned into a small jungle where the canopy blocked the sun's rays. A myriad of bright-colored flowers hung from the trees. After a short walk, we entered a clearing with a shimmering pool in its center. It mirrored the pool I had traveled through when I first entered Elswyth.

"Is this..." I began to ask.

"A portal?" Nera finished for me. When I nodded, she smiled and returned the gesture. "Long ago it was before I closed it off to keep this island safe. When your uncle first gained the crown, he found this place and asked me to grant him more power. I saw him for what he truly was and refused him. To ensure he could never return, I sealed this portal. However, the magic of Alari still exists within its waters. Now please strip and enter."

I did as she instructed and removed the slip dress I had awoken in. Once nude, I stepped into the water and found that it was very deep. Kicking my feet to stay afloat, I looked up at Nera.

She tilted her head up, and the sun illuminated her face. She chanted in a language I was not familiar with. The water slowly started to bubble. A tingling sensation spread through my body. Nera dropped her gaze down to me. "Calliope Mariana Delmari, Princess of Alari. What will you do with your powers once returned to you?"

"I will return to Caldor, defeat my uncle, and stop the rains from flooding this land."

"What if stopping the rains meant you could not return home? Would you stay here to help the humans or would you flee back to Alari, as if this land never existed?"

I never expected to have to stay here. All I wanted was to return home, to see my mother again. I hesitated for a moment before I answered. "I will stay. I could not leave these good people to drown."

A smile crossed Nera's face. "For centuries, the rulers of Alari have always been born in pairs. One to rule the realm of the mer, the other to protect this world from the wrath of the storms. It was your mother who was to come to Elswyth and Arik was to rule Alari. But your uncle was selfish. He wanted to keep your mother as a political bargain. Arik came to Elswyth to allow the storms to continue. When he arrived, he realized that once the storms continued, he could keep the realm of Elswyth for himself. He made a deal with the storm's spirit and the two became one. It took three long years, but the humans defeated him and stole the trident, he was unable to maintain the magic needed to keep the storm's powers. When he stole the gem from you, it gave him the power to reconnect with the storms." She knelt, so we met eye to eye. "Once your uncle is defeated. You will need to stay, to be able to keep the storm spirit away."

"What will happen in Alari if I stay? I have no twin to rule the realm in my absence."

Nera's smile grew. "Your mother will live a long and happy life. Before her time is over, there will be a new generation of the Delmari line to continue the cycle. Or should I say, *the Darksea line*?" She offered me a wink.

Heat rose to my cheeks. "Killian and I will not only be together but also have children?"

"As the way the future is currently written? Yes. But fear not, once balance is restored you will be able to visit Alari as you please. As will your children be able to visit you here in Elswyth. Do you agree to restore balance to the realms?"

"Yes. I will restore the balance. I will save Elswyth, Alari, and their peoples."

Nera offered me a nod and stood. Looking back to the sky, she continued her chant. When she was done, the bubbles vanished. I looked down, and instead of legs, my tail wadded in the water. "Thank you." Tears streamed down my face. I felt whole once again. Not only did I feel whole, I felt more. My magic felt stronger than it ever had. It flowed through my veins and sang in harmony with my body.

"You are so welcome, dear."

I pulled myself out of the pool, shifted into my human form, and stood. Now that my magic had been returned to me, I could easily switch between my two forms. Wrapping Nera in a hug, she nearly staggered back from the force. Once she steadied herself, she hugged me back.

"Do you need to rest another day before you return to your pirate?"

"Thank you for everything, but I must return as soon as I can. I cannot waste another moment."

"Then go, my child. Remember your promise. And, as long as it is held, you are welcome here anytime."

Without another word, I turned and sprinted toward the shore. Running into the ocean, the gentle waves splashed against my legs. Once deep enough, I transformed into my true form and swam as fast as I could to Caldor.

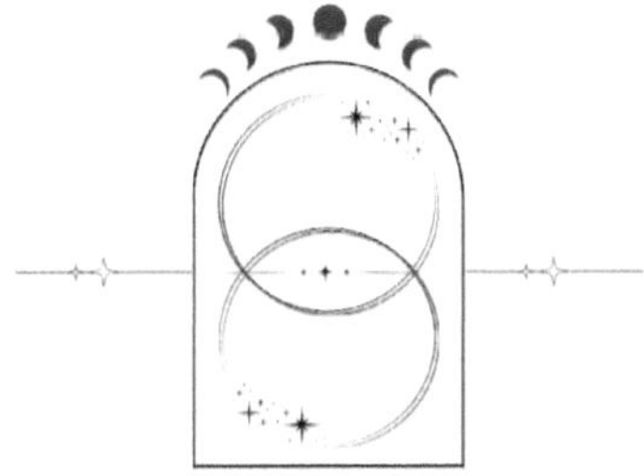

# Fourteen

When I entered the tavern, all eyes were on me. Killian's voice boomed through the crowd as he pushed past people to get to me, fury raged in his eyes. "Where have you been? Why would you leave without telling anyone?"

I rushed over to him, wrapped my arms around his neck, and pulled him into a kiss. He pulled away and gave me a look of confusion.

"I have my magic back!" I cried out.

"You what?" He asked in surprise.

"I can transform. I have my magic back!"

He offered a smile that did not meet his eyes. "So, this means you are returning home?"

"No!" I released him, took a step back, and hit him in the arm. "This means we have more of an even playing field with Arik. We can defeat him this time!"

"We will not be sending any more good people to die!" Van said from the bar. Killian and I turned to face him as he continued. "That's enough. There is no way we can defeat such a monster."

Hawk, who sat next to Van, nodded in agreement. "Killian, you have to stop this madness before you get us all killed!"

Murmurs filled the tavern. Some agreed with Van, some thought it was crazy to speak against the captain.

"Van," Killian growled. "If we don't stop him, we all will die. All of us. All human life will cease to exist!"

"I have gotten letters from family who traveled north to the capital. There is no storm there!" One of the pirates said.

"Don't you understand it will expand?" Killian asked.

Van stood and walked over to Killian. "Hawk and I are leaving. We refuse to die for this. Anyone who wants to join us is welcome." Van walked out of the bar, with Hawk and half of the crew following behind him.

The room stayed silent for too long after they left. Tension hung in the air. Killian looked around the room, seeing who stayed. "I will not ask you to put your lives on the line for this."

A woman named Jaki stood and walked over to us. "You and Vari took me in when I had nowhere to go. You both taught me I had worth beyond what others thought of me, beyond how others treated me. I will always lay my life down for you. Whatever you need."

It was then I realized that most who stayed were women. Vari had told me she had organized a part of the crew of survivors. To give them a home, to remind them of their strength.

A smile grew on my face. "Another man has tried to steal something away from us." As I began, all eyes were on me. "This time, we will not allow him to take from us. We will get our vengeance upon him. We will make him feel powerless and afraid. We will show no mercy, as he and so many others have refused to show us any." As the women cheered, I took Killian's hand in mine and smiled up at him. "I hope you have another ship because we are ready for war."

"I do, but it won't hold all of us. It only holds five."

"I will go!" Jaki said.

"We will too," shouted two sisters, Maria and Belle, from the back of the tavern.

Killian looked down at me. "Well, it appears you have your crew. What will you call yourselves?"

"The Vengeance of Alari. We leave at dawn."

"Aye, captain!" The three women and Killian responded.

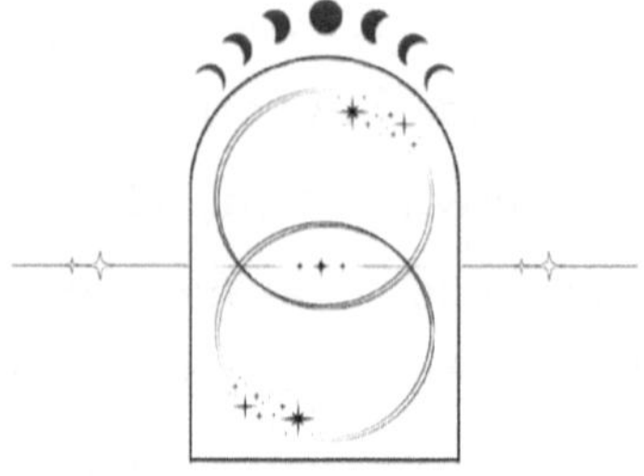

# Fifteen

We spent the day in each other's company. We did not know if this would be the last day we would have together. With dawn looming over us, we did not want to waste any time. After dinner, we all retreated to our rooms to rest. Killian took me by the hand and guided me into his bedroom. Once inside, he locked the door behind us. He glared down at me with a displeased look.

"What's wrong?" I questioned.

Killian let out a heavy sigh. "You left and did not even say goodbye." He dropped his gaze to the floor.

My eyes widened, and I staggered back. "You haven't spoken to me for days. When I heard the call of my people, I couldn't resist it! I couldn't waste any time!"

"Is that all I am to you?" He walked past me, not sparing me a glance. "A waste of time?"

"No!" I spun to face him. "Not at all." Grabbing his wrist, I pulled him to face me.

Tears misted his eyes. "I know we just met, but when I thought I lost you too, it broke me."

I wrapped him in a hug. "I am not going anywhere, Killian." I couldn't imagine leaving him, even before my promise to Nera.

"Won't you be returning to Alari once we defeat your uncle?" He pulled away from my embrace. His face and tone were cold as stone.

"No. I am going to stay here. I have a very important duty to uphold once Arik is gone. The goal is to return here with you once it is over."

His face softened as he looked down at me. "You want to stay here with me?" He raised an eyebrow.

"More than anything," I whispered.

Without another word, Killian stepped toward me, lifted me in the air, and planted his lips firmly on mine. Wrapping my arms and legs around him, I increased the passion in our kiss. My tongue pushed past his lips and danced with his. He tossed me onto the bed and offered me a predatory smirk.

"Shall we explore that beautiful human body of yours again, love?" He dragged his tongue across his top lip.

I sat up on my elbows and smiled. "Please. Make me forget about what lies ahead."

"Don't say another word," he commanded.

I nodded, and he quickly situated himself between my legs. Lifting my skirt, he ducked his head under it. Slipping my underwear off my body, he tossed them onto the floor. A moan escaped my lips as I felt his tongue slowly drag up my slit. Gripping onto the sheets, I tossed my head back from the pleasure. Killian's tongue pathed circles over my most delicate part. When he reached my clit, his tongue flicked over it, causing another moan to escape my lips.

Killian pulled his head out from under my skirt, licking my juices off his lips. "Gods, you are divine." He pulled himself to meet my lips and kissed me hungrily.

Reaching down, I gently stroked him through his pants. All I wanted was his considerable length deep inside me once again. "I need you," I moaned in between his kisses.

He pulled away, and my lips ached in his absence. "And you will have me, love." Quickly, he removed his pants and shirt and pulled up my skirt to reveal myself to him. Stepping forward, he lined himself up with my entrance. He slowly teased, leaving me craving more as he gently pushed his tip in and out of me.

"Killian, please. I need all of you," I pleaded.

"So eager." He offered me a smirk as he eased more of him inside me. Slowly, he thrust to allow me to adjust to his girth.

"Please," I continued to beg. It was all my body allowed me to do.

In one quick motion, Killian pushed himself deep inside, making me take him fully. I let out a scream of pleasure as he picked up the pace. Reaching forward, I grabbed him by the back of his head and pulled him in for another kiss. As we kissed, Killian ripped my dress off my body, leaving me bare for him.

Each time I thought I was going to reach my climax, he slowed, pulling me away from that ledge I was so desperate to cross. Over and over, he built my pleasure and brought me down just before I could explode from it. My body ached by the time he finally allowed me to find my pleasure. I let out a scream as stars filled my eyes. Clenching around his cock, I quivered around him.

Pushing deep inside me, Killian let out a groan as he found his release. Heat flooded my body. Holding himself there, it twitched inside me as all of his essence shot into me. When he pulled out I was left with an emptiness, as if my soul ached to be intertwined with his.

"I am glad you're staying here," Killian smirked down at me.

"Why is that?"

"Because, even if you wanted to, I would never let you leave." He leaned down and planted a kiss on my forehead.

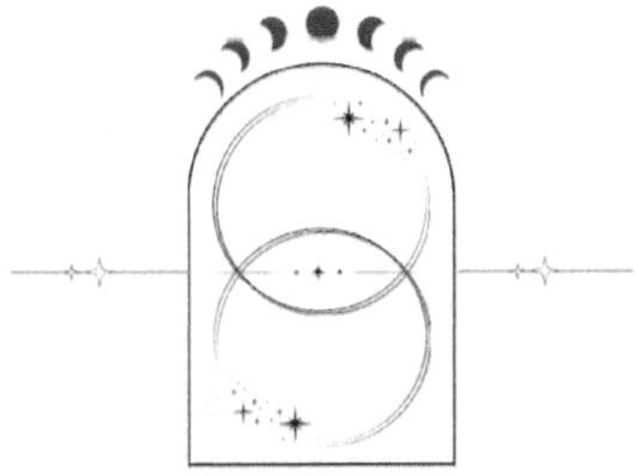

# Sixteen

At dawn, the five of us were aboard the small ship and headed to the island where it all began. The sea was calm, and the air was filled with the sound of the rain falling into the ocean. Pacing back and forth on the top deck, I tapped my fingers against each other over and over. I did not know if or when my uncle would show himself, which left me and my crew feeling on edge.

This time, I would be ready for him. This time, I would get vengeance for what he had done to me, the lands of Alari and Elswyth, and my friends.

Killian stood at the helm with his gaze focused on the small deserted island off in the distance. After I walked over to him, he looked down at me and gave me a smile that did not reach his eyes. I thought back to the first time I had laid my eyes on him, and how confident he looked then. Even though he wore the same red outfit today, and had the trident strapped to his back, most of that confidence had been washed away by the never-ending rains.

"How are you feeling?" he asked.

"Nervous." I could not lie. My magic felt so much stronger than it ever had. Even when the source of my magic was the Gem I did not have this much power flowing through my veins. Still, I needed to be cautious. I could only imagine how much power the Gem gave Arik. "Nervous, but ready."

Killian turned his gaze out toward the sea. "Calliope," he said nearly in a whisper, "I am sorry. When I first found you on the island, I underestimated you. I should not have done that. Neither should your uncle. Luckily, I corrected my mistake before it was too late."

"I won't give Arik the chance to make that same mistake," I snarled. Turning away from Killian, I looked out at the ocean in the direction of Nera's island. A smile crossed my face as I saw a familiar and comforting golden flash on the horizon. Never would I forget the kindness she had shown me. In my time of need, the mother of mer was there for me. I would not disappoint her.

The winds picked up as we got closer to the island. As we anchored, I expected Arik would have attacked by now, but he had still not made an appearance. Boarding a small boat, Killian and I both rowed to the island. The three women we brought with us stayed on board, just in case.

When we reached the shore, Killian jumped out of the boat and pushed it onto the beach. Taking my hand, he helped me up and out to stand at his side.

My gaze was fixed on the rocks just down the shoreline. The tattoo on my leg stung from the memory of me slipping, scraping my skin, and bleeding into the ocean. My eyes widened, and I inhaled sharply as I realized what had happened. Was it my blood that awoke him? Is that how Arik knew I had traveled through the portal to this island? A chill ran down my spine.

"Are you alright?" Killian asked.

I offered a small nod. "Give me your dagger," I commanded.

With a raised eyebrow, he unsheathed the dagger from his waist and handed it to me, handle first. Taking the dagger, I turned to face the ocean.

"Arik Tristian Delmari," I called out. "Let us settle this in the old ways. I call upon you for a blood duel. Face me." I sliced into my palm and allowed my blood to drip into the sea. "Are you willing to lay down your life for your cause? I am willing to take you down for mine."

"Calliope, what are you doing?!" Killian grabbed me, pulled me against him, and snatched the knife from my hand. A mix of anger and confusion was on his face as he stared down at me.

The rain abruptly stopped, but the dark clouds still loomed. A rumble filled the air as the earth quaked, causing me to fall into Killian as we both staggered from the tremor. Before us, the ocean parted and created high walls of water. The sea floor was now bare, and the kelp lay limp on the sand. Arik walked toward us with a cocky grin on his face. His red tentacles lurked behind his back, poised, and ready to strike. The clouds parted, and the sun hit his face, illuminating his golden hair and blue eyes. Slowly, he clapped as he walked toward us.

This man thought himself to be a god.

"I am surprised you were able to make it all the way back here without alerting me and had to use your blood to summon me. I must say, I am delighted to learn it is still as sweet, even after I took your magic. I hope there are no hard feelings about that, dear niece. I did what had to be done." He stopped about halfway between us, a wall of ocean behind him. "I hope you do not plan on begging for your magic back. I cannot allow you to have it. I also cannot let you return home and report to my brat of a sister that I am still alive. The last time I faced her, I barely made it out alive. However, If I faced her again, the outcome would be very different. I don't want to have to kill all of my remaining family."

Killian gripped my shoulder but did not say a word. This was my fight. He promised me he would let me have my moment.

I let out a chuckle. "It is not my mother you need to fear, but you are still correct. This time, it will end differently. You won't make it out alive."

"Foolish girl," Arik snarled in response. His gaze flicked toward Killian, and his eyes widened. "It seems you brought me another gift. After I took the Gem, I never expected you to bring me the trident." He raised his hand, and the center of his forehead glowed red. The Gem of Alari had been implanted under the skin. Arik raised his hand and extended his fingers toward the trident. Anger contorted his face as nothing happened. Slowly, he clenched his hand into a fist so tight the whites of his knuckles showed.

Stepping to my side, Killian wielded the trident. "Sorry, the gods have a different idea about who should wield this." As if on command, lightning struck down, hitting the forks, and filled them with electric power.

Arik's eyes darkened and the walls of the parted sea slammed shut. Just like that, he was gone, and the rains returned. Taking a step forward, I extended my arms and waved my hands through the air to part the sea where Arik had been. Only, where I was expecting to see the corpse of a mer or man, a single fish flopped on the sand. Releasing my hold on the ocean I let out a scream. I could not let him escape. I ran out into the ocean, transformed, and swam out into the dark waters.

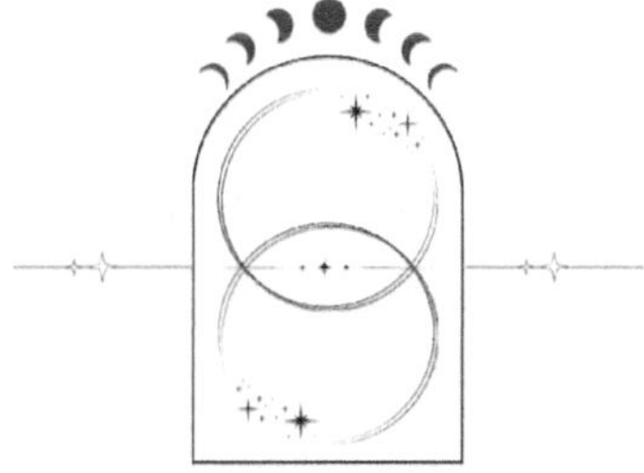

# Seventeen

White coral reefs were scattered about the seafloor. Only a few fish were seen while I searched for Arik. A chill ran through me. Coral reefs were meant to be full of color and life. Whatever Arik had done to these waters, destroyed them. There was no way I would be able to search this entire ocean for him. Sitting on a rock, I allowed a sweet melody to escape my lips. I hoped the sound would lure him directly to me, but there was no response. Again, I sang the melody, this time louder than before. I continued to raise my voice until I was sure the entire ocean heard my call, but I was greeted by silence.

Rage boiled within me as I swam back to the island. How could he have gotten away? How could I *let* him get away? I knew that was not the last time I would see him, but it did not ease the anger within me. Arik Delmari needed to die.

When I got back to the island, I transformed into my human form and walked onto the beach. Looking around, I was not able to see Killian. The small wooden boat was still beached, so I knew he should still be here. I hoped he was not too mad at me for swimming off into the sea after my uncle. As I walked the shoreline, worry filled me.

"Killian?" I called out. There was no response. "Killian!" I screamed, but my voice was lost in the sound of the strong winds and rain.

It was then that I heard a grunt coming from the center of the island. Turning, I ran toward the sound. Next to the pool of water that housed the portal to Alari, Killian laid too still in the sand that was now stained red. The trident was still gripped tightly in his hand. Arik loomed in front of him with the look of victory on his face.

My stomach turned. No, was I too late? By leaving, did I allow Killian to be killed? A tentacle reached down and tried to grab onto the trident. An electric shock went through it, causing it to jolt back to its owner. The bright red tentacle was now a dull burnt color.

"You will have to let it go at some point, you worthless pirate," Arik snarled down at Killian.

Killian finally raised his head, smirking up at my uncle. Relief filled me as the sound of his voice hit my ears. Not dead. The man I loved was still alive. "Over my dead body," he said weakly, blood leaking from his lips.

Arik kicked Killian in his side, forcing him to toss onto his back. He let out a wince in response.

"That can be arranged," Arik growled.

Before Arik could do anything else, I called upon the water from the pool to rise and force him away from Killian. Taken off guard, my uncle flew back several feet. I stepped out from the dune grass. "The only dead body that will be here today is yours."

"Ah, so the little mermaid returns. Tell me, how did you get your tail back?" Arik snapped at me.

"Nera," I said coldly.

Anger flashed in Arik's eyes. "No, she hates the people of Alari. She would never help you!"

"It is *you* she hates. For you spit in the face of the gifts she has given us." Walking over to Killian, I reached down and gently took the trident from his grasp. "Go," I whispered. "Go back to the ship. Get the girls out of here." Killian did not argue with me. He struggled to stand, but once he was on his feet, he pulled me into a firm swift kiss. When he pulled away he gave me a quick nod before he limped away. All I wanted was for him to be safe. I would not let him die here. Focusing my attention back to Arik, I hardened my gaze. "It is I who will guard the oceans of Elswyth and keep the spirit of the storm at bay. I will make Nera and The Mother proud of me, proud of Alari, and proud of its people. You are nothing more than a small obstacle in my path."

"You are so naïve. How did Ariella raise such a foolish child? Don't you see? There is only one way this will end." A tentacle shot out at me.

I inhaled deeply and mimicked one of the moves Killian taught me when he was training me with the trident. The prongs jabbed into the tentacle, pierced it, and black blood spilled onto the sand. The appendage recoiled back to its master.

Over and over, tentacles lunged for me, and I fought them off with the trident. I was able to get one pinned to the ground and send a bolt of electricity through it. When I went to pull the trident out, it stuck. As I gave it a second pull, another tentacle came at me. It smacked into my side and caused me to fall into the pool of water. The force was so hard that I sank deep into the pool, and I was on the other side of the portal. The warm waters of my homeland greeted me. I secured my grip on the trident and kicked my feet to swim back up to the surface.

When I emerged, Arik was at the edge, waiting for me. "Stupid girl. That was your one chance to return home and live."

Using my magic, I forced the water to shoot me out of the pool, where I landed behind Arik. Before he could spin to face me, I thrusted the trident into the spot on his back where the tentacles emerged. Arik let out a scream. He pulled away from me and used his tentacles to rush across the sand to get some distance between us.

"You bitch!" He screamed as he looked down at the blood-covered sand.

The water of the portal bubbled, and both of our attentions focused on it. Not even a second later, my mother emerged from the water. Rage contorted her face as she glared down at me. Despite the anger, she looked perfect, as she always did. Her long hair was in a braid, wrapped around the crown of her head. Even out of water, she did not have a single hair out of place. I wondered what she thought of her daughter, who was covered in blood and sand.

"Hello, brother," she snarled at Arik before her intense glare shot at me. "Always too curious for your own good, but, I knew this day would come."

"Sister, return to your castle and take your brat with you! This world is mine."

"No, this realm is the humans. Do not disrupt the balance. Not everything is yours for the taking." Mother slowly looked back toward Arik. "Return the Gem, and allow me to take both it and the trident to its rightful home."

"You will need to rip it out of my cold, dead body."

"That can be arranged," I heard three female voices say in unison. Turning, I saw my crew, each with a weapon in hand.

"You humans think you can defeat me? I am the monster that has haunted your seas for decades."

"Enough!" Forcing the power of voice into my scream, I hoped to render my uncle helpless. Arik covered his ears and scrunched his face. The four women did not react to my high-pitched cry. My voice brought him down to his knees and blood leaked from his ears. Never would I allow him to silence me again. Arik would feel my wrath and the pain he caused me. A smile crossed my lips as I watched Killian sneaking up behind Arik. Though still with a slight limp, he seemed to be much better than before.

"What are you smiling at?" Arik snarled.

"The fact you let a worthless pirate get the upper hand," Killian said as he ran a blade through Arik's tentacles, severing them from his body.

They all dropped to the ground, squirting black blood and twitching several times before becoming motionless.

"No!" Arik screamed. He looked down frantically at the parts of him lying on the ground. I thought back to

Vari and the story she told, wondering if this was what he looked like after she had cut off that man's weapon.

While Arik was distracted, I rushed toward him and thrust the trident into his stomach. Lightning shot from the trident, electrocuting my uncle. When I removed the trident, Arik fell to the ground, and I watched the light leave his eyes. Killian ran toward me, pulling me away from my uncle's lifeless body. Pushing away from him, I took the dagger off his belt, knelt, and made a small cut into Arik's forehead, where I saw that glowing red light. Once the opening was wide enough, The Gem popped right out. Taking it, I placed it in the small indent of the trident's head. Once in place, it flashed a bright red light before going dark.

Immediately, the rains stopped, the sky cleared, and I felt the warmth of the sun on my skin.

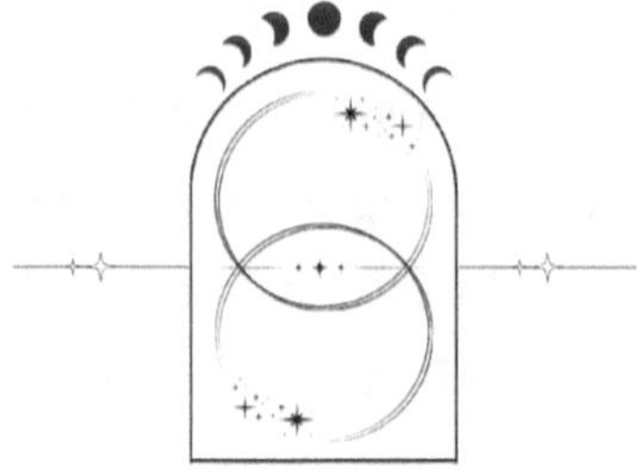

# Eighteen

Two weeks later, the ocean retreated to its former levels. No longer were the homes of Caldor flooded, though they had sustained much damage. Killian and the remaining crew helped restore a lot of the damaged homes. He continued to offer the tavern to anyone who needed a place to stay during the repairs, even the mayor.

Several of the Darksea pirates had returned to Caldor and apologized to Killian for leaving. Being the kind man he was under all that armor around his heart, he understood and welcomed them back.

For the first time since defeating Arik, we were all on a ship, headed back toward the island. The entire time, I sat on the top deck, behind the helm, soaking in the sun's rays. Killian and I, once again, boarded the lifeboat and rowed to the sandy shore of the island.

There, Nera and my mother waited for us.

"Calliope, maybe now you can formally introduce me to your human companion?" My mother offered a smile toward him.

Killian bowed. "Hello, your majesty. I am glad we are meeting in better circumstances. My name is Killian Darksea."

"Darksea?" She raised her eyebrow.

Nera let out a chuckle.

"Yes," he nodded.

"Well, that is not a name I have heard in a long time. Not since before..." My mother's gaze wandered, and her voice trailed off.

"You have heard of the Darksea name? How?" I questioned.

"Because the Darkseas were once a powerful family in Alari," Nera finally spoke. "But they traveled here, with your uncle, all those years ago."

"That's impossible. My grandfather fought Arik and tried to stop him!"

"That is true. Your grandfather did not know what Arik was doing before it was too late. Arik had brought over several powerful families from Alari. Your grandfather was the only one who survived after Arik harvested their magic."

"That means..." I struggled to force the words out as I looked at Killian. "You're part mer?"

"Oh, thank The Mother," my mother sighed. "I was worried about having a human son-in-law."

Killian looked at my mother with wide eyes, then back to me.

"No need to fret," Nera continued. "Besides, today we are here to bestow Calliope with her title and gifts. We can teach the pirate about how to access his tail another time."

My mother took my hand and guided me back to the portal, and Nera and Killian followed us. An altar made of coral and seashells had been placed in front of the pool. On top, it sat a crown of shells and sea glass.

Walking over to the altar, Nera stopped just before it. "Kneel, child."

Stepping to face her, I did as she commanded.

She raised her gaze to the sky and spoke in a language I was not familiar with. Slowly, she looked down at me. "Calliope Mariana Delmari, do you agree to protect the seas of Elswyth and keep the spirit of the storm from returning?"

"I do," I said with every ounce of confidence I had. For the first time, I felt right. I felt at home. Looking over to Killian, I smiled. This was where I was meant to be.

Nera placed the crown on my head and chanted once again. Heat washed over my body, but was gone just as quickly as it arrived. "Rise my child. You have made Mother proud." She bent down and gently kissed my forehead.

I stood, and as soon as I was on my two feet, my mother wrapped me in a tight embrace. "I hate leaving you a realm away. Please promise me you will visit?"

"I promise." I hugged her back tightly. The feelings of guilt about leaving lingered in my mind. How could I ever think it was her that was the villain?

Nera slowly walked over to Killian. "Do you want to unlock your true self, boy?"

He hesitated for a moment, looked at me, then back to Nera. "Yes."

"Get in the water." She pointed to the pool.

He did as instructed, and Nera repeated the same ritual she did while I was on her island. The water bubbled around where he swam and once it was over, Killian no longer had legs but a bright red tail with golden sparkles.

With wide eyes, he smiled up at me. "It is all clear now." He got out of the pool and transformed back to his legged form.

"Return to your town. Though the war is over, there is still much work to be done," Nera said.

I gave both mother and Nera a final goodbye before walking back to our small boat. When we reached the shore, I looked up at Killian and smiled.

"Want to swim back?" I questioned.

Killian offered me the brightest smile. "Absolutely."

With that, the two of us ran into the ocean, transformed into our mer form, and swam home.

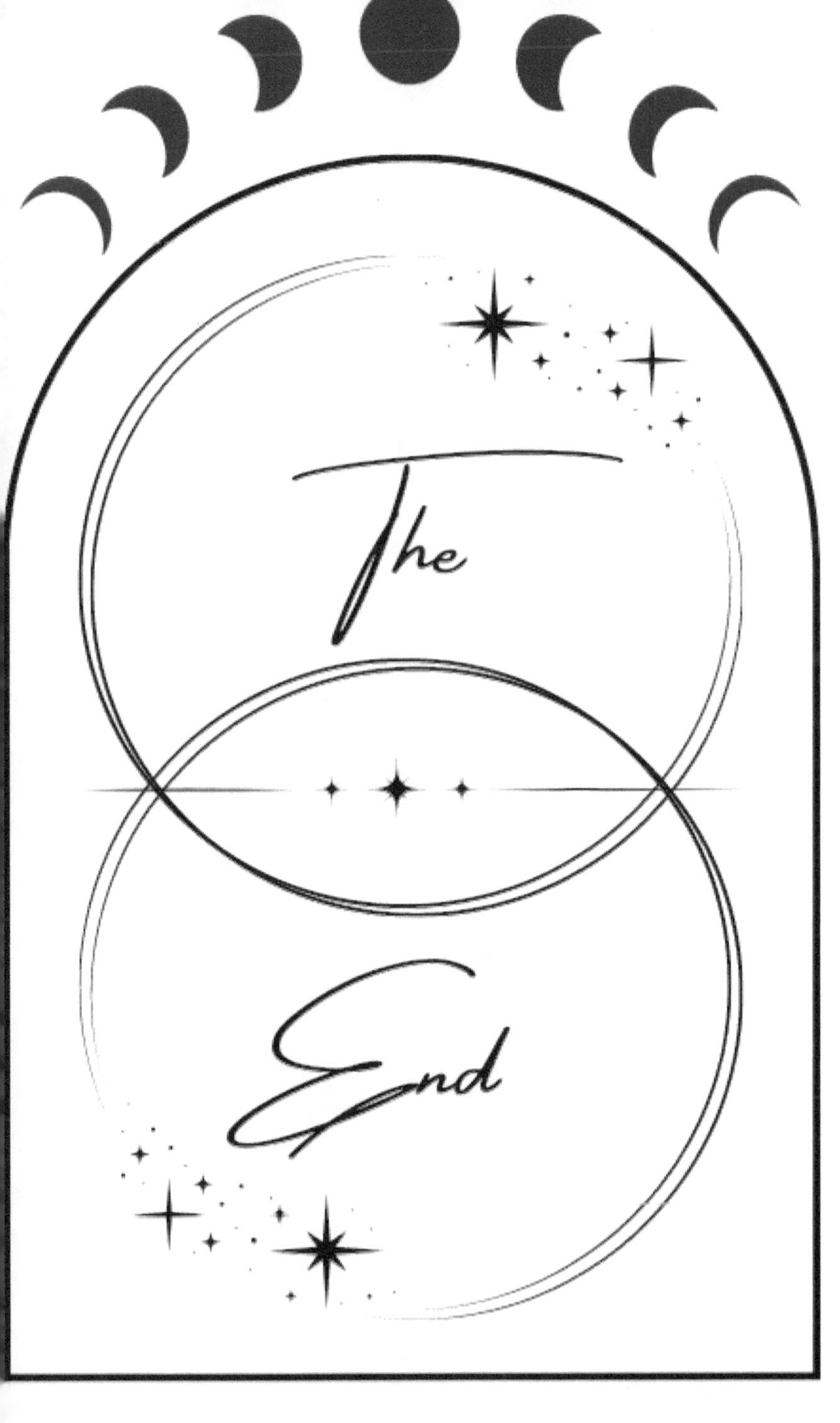
The
End

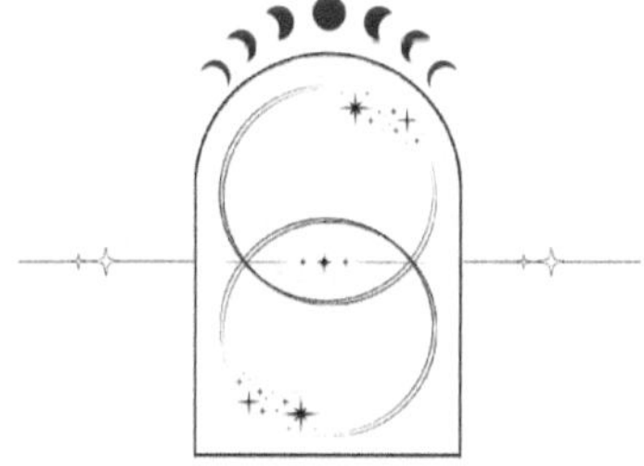

# Also by Willow Asteria

The Blood Singer Trilogy
https://amzn.to/3KO4erc

The Realms of Elswyth
https://amzn.to/3xsvM2r

*Learn More Here!*

www.ingramcontent.com/pod-product-compliance
Lightning Source LLC
Chambersburg PA
CBHW020046310726
48970CB00007B/2428